Date Due

'I have everything I need.'

'Not quite,' he said softly. 'You're still denying yourself the right to an adult relationship.'

'I have to, David. I can't allow myself to get close to anyone because it makes me vulnerable, and I can't let that happen. Not again.'

For a long time he stood there looking at her, then he drew her into his arms and hugged her gently. 'I won't hurt you. Either of you. I promise that. You can back off at any time. But, please, give us a chance. We could have something so special here, Julia. Something lasting. Don't close the door on it without knowing what it is you're walking away from.'

He kissed her, just a feathering of his lips across her forehead, and then he turned and strode down the hall, picking up his coat on the way, and she heard the soft click of the front door behind him.

It was the loneliest sound in the world.

Caroline Anderson has the mind of a butterfly. She's been a nurse, a secretary, a teacher, run her own soft-furnishing business and now she's settled on writing. She says, 'I was looking for that elusive something. I finally realised it was variety, and now I have it in abundance. Every book brings new horizons and new friends, and in between books I have learned to be a juggler. My teacher husband John and I have two beautiful and talented daughters, Sarah and Hannah, umpteen pets and several acres of Suffolk that nature tries to reclaim every time we turn our backs!' Caroline also writes for the Mills & Boon® Tender Romance™ series.

Recent titles by the same author:

ACCIDENTAL RENDEZVOUS
RESCUING DR RYAN
A MOTHER BY NATURE
GIVE ME FOREVER

THE PERFECT CHRISTMAS

BY
CAROLINE ANDERSON

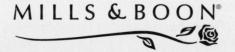

MILLS & BOON®

*MILLS & BOON and
MILLS & BOON with the Rose Device
are registered trademarks of the publisher.*

*First published in Great Britain 2001
Large Print edition 2002
Harlequin Mills & Boon Limited,
Eton House, 18-24 Paradise Road,
Richmond, Surrey TW9 1SR*

© Caroline Anderson 2001

ISBN 0 263 17176 0

*Set in Times Roman 16½ on 18 pt.
17-0602-47381*

*Printed and bound in Great Britain
by Antony Rowe Ltd, Chippenham, Wiltshire*

CHAPTER ONE

JULIA glanced at her watch and sighed, her fingers tapping on the steering wheel. She was going to be late on the ward—and today, of all days, with a new consultant surgeon starting, an operations list a mile long and new admissions that had come in over the weekend to sort out.

Something had obviously happened at the roundabout up ahead, bringing the traffic, such as it was, to a grinding halt on the inner ring road. Another minor shunt, probably. It was always happening. If only she'd left earlier, but Katie had been difficult and it was a miracle she was here even now. She glanced at her watch again. It was ten to seven, and if they didn't get moving in the next couple of minutes, she would definitely be late.

She peered ahead into the winter darkness and wished it was daylight so she could see what was going on. If she could only creep forward a little further, she could take the side road and cut through to the hospital that way, but if there were any casualties, she really ought to go and help.

Torn between her various obligations, she hesitated for a moment, but then someone's headlights picked up a running figure darting from car to car, calling out. With a sinking feeling she opened her door and stood up, half out of the car, and the man saw her and ran towards her. 'Got any first-aid experience?' he asked. 'One of the drivers is bleeding badly.'

'I'm a nurse,' she replied, resigning herself to being late. She squeezed her car off the road, locked it and ran towards the roundabout, arriving at the scene just as a solidly built man wrenched open the door of one of the cars and stuck his head inside.

'Where's the casualty?' she asked the man who'd hailed her, and he pointed at the person who'd just opened the door.

'In there. It's a woman. That man's just got the door open—it was jammed.'

'Can someone call the ambulances?' she said, heading for the car at a run, and several people confirmed that it had been done already. Good. Hopefully they'd soon be here and she could get on her way.

Tucking her long fair hair behind her ears, she leant over the man who was obstructing her view of the driver. All she could see was a pair of massive shoulders filling the gap, but the smell of blood was unmistakable. 'Excuse me,' she said, but he didn't move, so she tried again, firming up her voice and injecting more authority. 'Can you let me see her? I'm a nurse.'

He lifted his head a fraction and turned it, and she caught a glimpse of a strong profile in the reflected streetlight before he spoke, his voice deep and calm and confident. 'A nurse? Excellent. I'm a doctor—you can give me a hand. I can't let go of this one—her necklace is embedded in her throat and I think she's nicked her carotid artery judging by the way she's pumping blood out all over me. She reeks of alcohol as well—I think she's been partying. Whatever, I can't let go of her neck and her passenger's injured, too. Can you check him?'

'Sure,' she agreed, glad someone who knew what they were doing was in charge of the bleeding woman. 'What about the people in the other cars? Have you seen any of them?'

'I think they're out and walking around— more shaken up than anything. These two were definitely going faster, judging by the damage to the car and the position of it.'

As she made her way to the passenger side of the car, Julia glanced around. Two people were wandering around looking dazed, staring at their damaged vehicle. It was by the central island of the roundabout, its front quarter smashed, and the car with the injured driver had obviously cut in front of it and was half up the roundabout's grassy centre, the remains of a road sign jutting out from under the bonnet. It had clearly come to an abrupt halt, and it looked as if the driver just simply hadn't seen the roundabout coming.

Two other cars were slewed across the roundabout, adding to the confusion, but the damage to them was slight and the occupants were obviously all right.

She tugged open the passenger door and checked the other occupant of the first car. He was groggy but conscious, bleeding from a cut on his forehead and clutching his knees and moaning. No seat belt, she noticed, and wondered how on earth he hadn't just gone straight through the windscreen. She looked up at her impromptu colleague just as he lifted his head, and her eyes were caught by his, strangely piercing, like sunlight through rain. Her own eyes were grey, but not like that! Not that amazing grey that was almost silver. They took her breath away.

'Knees and head,' she told him after a moment, trying to concentrate, and he nodded.

'Don't think he had a belt on—idiot. He's lucky to be alive. How's his spine?'

'Suspect, I should think,' she said, eyeing the man's crouched position on the edge of the seat. He was slumped at a strange angle, but at least he could feel his knees. He might not think so just at the moment, but that was definitely a good sign.

A siren sounded in the distance, and the paramedics ran up to them. The doctor detailed his findings, Julia did the same, and within a few minutes their patients were handed over and whisked away. Another ambulance had arrived and was checking out the people from the other cars, and the police asked Julia and her companion if they'd seen anything.

'It had happened when I arrived,' she told them, and they took her name and address and let her go. She ran back to her car, wiped her hands on a rag she used for the windscreen and drove to the hospital by the back route, abandoned her car in the car park and arrived on her ward, bloodstained and grubby, a mere half-hour late.

'What on earth have you been doing?' the night sister asked, eyeing her in amazement.

Julia snorted. 'Roadside rescue,' she said succinctly. 'Give me a minute to change into my spare uniform and have a quick scrub, and I'll be with you.'

In fact, it was only her coat that was bloodstained. Her tunic top had escaped, and her trousers were only slightly damp on the knees from kneeling on the road. Still, she changed completely, scrubbing her hands thoroughly just to be on the safe side before going back to the office.

'Here,' the night sister said, putting a cup of tea into her hand, and she took it gratefully and buried her nose in it.

'Oh, gorgeous, Angie, thanks,' she said with a smile. 'It's really chilly out there.'

'Was that the cause, do you think?'

Julia wrinkled her nose. 'Maybe. She might have skidded on a little patch of ice, but I think it's unlikely. Judging from the fact that she reeked of booze, there was probably another reason.'

'Good grief. It's only the first of December! Are they getting into the spirit of Christmas this soon?'

'Some people only need the slightest excuse,' she said grimly, and concentrated on her tea instead of thinking about Andrew and another frosty night nearly four years ago—

'So, how was the weekend?' she asked. 'Lots of admissions?'

'Wouldn't you know? It's been bedlam, apparently. We had six surgical emergencies and three RTAs last night alone. We haven't got them all, but ICU is chocka and they're stacked up in Resus.'

Julia rolled her eyes and sighed. 'Oh, yum. One of those days.'

'Absolutely. And we've got the new boy starting shortly, lord help us all—if he ever gets here. He said he'd be here by seven, and he's late, too. Maybe he came the same way.'

'Well, if he did he'll be stuck in the queue, because the roundabout's blocked solid. I'm only here because I know the back way.'

'Great. We've had a call from A and E to stand by for an RTA victim with a deep incision in the neck—could that be yours? If it is, I hope this Armstrong guy gets here soon, because Nick Sarazin's just phoned in with flu and Armstrong's next in line, so he'd better be up to speed, because she's punctured her carotid, apparently, and they've just tacked her together in A and E pending a proper job.'

Just then there was a knock on the door, and she looked up straight into a pair of familiar rainwashed eyes. Her heart slammed against her ribs, and he smiled in recognition and came into the room. He'd shed his coat and changed his shirt, but his temple still carried a little streak of blood beneath the floppy dark hair.

Her eyes scanned him in the second it took him to cross the room towards her, absorbing the fact that he looked less chunky without the padded jacket. He was still broad, but with a lithe muscularity that spoke of great strength. His broad, capable hand was extended in greeting, and his voice sent shivers down her spine.

'Hi, there. We meet again. David Armstrong.'

Their new consultant, a man she'd work with on a daily basis. Her heart gave a little jiggle of delight, but she ignored it, struggling for a measured response.

'Julia Revell. I'm the ward sister. Welcome aboard.'

She took his hand, the fingers cool and hard, the palm warm and dry and firm. A confident hand, strong and yet gentle. She felt a strange kind of helplessness creep over her, an urge to crawl into his arms and let him take away all her problems.

Not that she had many problems. Not if you didn't count the bills that were waiting to be paid, and the fact that Katie wasn't feeling too well and really, really hadn't wanted to go to the childminder or school this morning, and the car was overdue for servicing and her wardrobe was looking distinctly ragged.

Still, there was always the lottery.

She realised she was still holding his hand, the handshake now extended beyond mere convention, and with a tiny shake she pulled herself together and released him, stepping back. 'This is Angie Featherstone, our night sister. Angie, Mr Armstrong's the doctor I was telling you about at the RTA—last seen holding a pressure pad to a young woman's neck.'

He gave a wry grimace, his eyes crinkling with humour. 'Yes—in at the deep end. She's coming up to Theatre and guess who's on take all of a sudden? So it looks as if I get to do the follow-through on my good Samaritan act. Can we squeeze her in or shall I tell her it's not convenient?'

Julia laughed and looked at Angie for confirmation. 'Can we?'

'There's always the corridor,' she said drily. 'Anyway, I'm out of here in a minute. I'll leave you to sort it out. I would suggest some rapid shuffling and a little emergency discharge. Talk to Nick Sarazin's registrar—one or two of his are looking pretty bright.'

'Good,' Julia said with feeling. 'We could use freeing up. OK, we'll stand by to take her shortly.'

He grinned. 'Right. I'd better go and get scrubbed up. I'll see you again later.'

He went out and closed the door, and Angie looked at Julia and sighed theatrically. 'Oh, what a luscious man. What did we do to get so lucky? Did you *see* those eyes?'

Oh, yes—and the strong, safe, capable hands, Julia thought, but it was only a thought, and that was all it could ever be. Never again, she'd vowed all those years ago, and it would take more than eyes the colour of an April storm and a touch that made her long for more to undermine that resolve. She straightened her shoulders and arched a brow at her colleague.

'I thought you were married?' she said drily, but Angie just laughed.

'I am—but you'd have to be dead to fail to notice a man like that—and don't tell me you didn't notice him, because I'll know you're lying.'

Julia shrugged, suppressing her interest. 'So he's good-looking,' she said dismissively. 'Lots of men are. I don't mix business and pleasure.'

Angie shot her a curious look. 'Did I suggest you should?'

She felt colour brush her cheeks, and sighed inwardly. 'Just setting the record straight. Let's get this report out of the way and I can start shuffling patients,' she said, clutching at normality. Anyway, she thought, her mind still running on the same track, he was bound to be married. All the decent men were, and most of the indecent ones, too. Not that she was interested, even if he was available.

Busy, that was what she needed to be—too busy to think straight, so there wasn't time to worry about David Armstrong and his broad shoulders and powerful hands and gorgeous eyes...

There was an old saying—be careful what you wish for, you might get it.

By the time she clocked off at three, Julia was deeply regretting her wish to be busy. They'd been rushed off their feet all day, and it was only at three thirty, when she'd done the handover and was in her car on the way to pick Katie up from school, that she realised just how tired she was.

Not just from today, but from every day, from the relentless passage of the days, one after the other, each with their own special problems.

If only she could stop worrying about the money, but there never seemed to be enough, not with Andrew's debts still to clear. Still, another three months and the credit-card bill would be paid, and maybe then things would be easier.

She pulled up outside the school and went in to retrieve Katie from the homework class she joined for the few minutes she had to wait each day. Sometimes it was more than a few minutes, but Julia was very wary about leaving her too long and shaking her confidence.

It had taken enough of a battering when Andrew had died.

'Mummy! Mummy, look what I did!'

'Hello, darling—oh, gorgeous! We'll stick it up on the fridge when it's dry.'

She fielded the wet painting, threw a distracted smile of thanks at the teacher supervising the little group and headed for the cloakroom with Katie to find her coat. It was wet and muddy—she'd been pushed over at lunchtime and had sat in a puddle, but she seemed quite unmoved by it.

'Why didn't you tell the dinner ladies?' Julia asked, wondering about the incident. 'They would have dried it for you.'

'Doesn't matter,' Katie said airily. 'Can we go? I want a drink.'

Was she being evasive? No. Julia told herself not to go into overdrive about bullying. It was probably just a casual bump, more than likely an accident.

'It'll be dry by tomorrow. Here, borrow my jumper so you don't get cold and then you won't have to wear your coat while it's still wet. Are you feeling better now?'

Katie nodded. 'School was fun today. We did singing.'

'That was nice.' She bundled her daughter up in her sweater, put her coat back on and headed for the car, damp coat and damper painting in hand. The sleeves of the jumper were trailing almost to the ground, and Katie skipped along, swinging them and laughing and looking quite unconcerned.

Not bullied, thank God.

Julia sighed with relief. It was sometimes so hard being a single parent and keeping things in perspective. She drove them home, made a simple meal of pasta and vegetables baked in the oven with grated cheese on top, and they sat together and watched children's TV while it browned, and then read Katie's book for a while after supper.

By seven thirty, when the little girl was tucked up in bed and the house was tidied, Julia was wiped out. She poured herself a small glass of wine from the bottle in the fridge, sat down in front of the television for a little relaxation and promptly fell asleep, waking much later with a wet lap and a crick in her neck.

She looked at her watch in disbelief. It was nearly ten, and she'd slept through the only programme she liked. Typical. With a wry grimace she put the now empty wineglass down, turned off the television, had a quick bath and went to bed, expecting to fall into a sound sleep instantly.

Oh, no. Her mind, slightly refreshed by the doze on the sofa, had no intention of letting her escape that easily. Instead it spooled endlessly through the events of the day, starting with the accident in the morning, then her next meeting with David Armstrong on the ward, then his visits later to check on his post-ops.

Every time he'd seen her he'd smiled that eye-crinkling smile, and she'd turned to putty. His shoulders had brushed against hers at someone's bedside and her heart had nearly stopped. He's just a man, she'd told herself, and now, lying in bed, she reminded herself of this again.

He's just a man.

And that, of course, was the root of the problem, because a man was what she wanted, what she needed in her life. Just a man, an ordinary, everyday decent human being to share life's ups and downs.

Or cause them. Every down that had happened to her in the past six years had been caused by Andrew.

No, she didn't want a man. Well, she did, but she didn't *need* a man. What she needed was sleep, so she could get up in the morning and do her job properly and not get the sack!

But her restless mind wouldn't let go, and when it did, it was only so that it could torture her with dreams...

'Hi, there.'

Julia looked up from her computer terminal at the work station, a smile of welcome already on her lips. Oh, heavens, she thought dizzily, the dreams didn't do his eyes justice.

She pulled herself together and tried to look professional instead of like a mesmerised rabbit. 'Morning. You're in bright and early.'

'I wanted to check my post-ops before my clinic at nine, and I need time to read through the notes before then, and I need to meet my secretary and have more than a five-second conversation with her at some time before the clinic, so—'

'You got up at five to make an early start.'

David laughed. 'Something like that. I don't suppose there's a kettle anywhere on the ward, is there? I'd like to chat about a couple of the patients with you. Besides, I only had time for a quick slug of tea before I left home, and I'm parched.'

'Have you had breakfast?' she asked, wondering what his wife thought about him leaving home so early and telling herself it was none of her business.

'You sound just like my mother,' he said with a slow smile that messed up her heart rhythm again, 'and, no, I didn't have time for breakfast either.'

'Better have some toast, then, to go with your tea—or was it coffee?'

'Tea sounds good.'

He followed her into the little kitchen, his broad shoulders and deep chest somehow filling the space and crowding her, but not unpleasantly. She felt…odd, as if his aura was brushing up against hers, chafing softly against it and sending little shivers up and down her spine.

She filled the kettle and switched it on, then turned and bumped into him, and he smiled and moved back a little. 'Sorry,' she said a touch breathlessly. 'It's rather cramped in here.'

'It's a nice cosy little retreat,' he corrected, the smile playing around his mouth and drawing an answering smile to her lips.

'It can be, but not for long. We're too busy usually to take advantage, but yesterday's bedlam seems to have retreated a bit.'

'Just as well, isn't it? You were running at full stretch, I would have thought.'

'We were a bit overcrowded. Still, with Nick off with flu we should be able to catch up a little. Two slices, or more?'

'Two to start with,' he said, and propped his hips against the units, his hands resting on the worktop each side so that his suit jacket gaped open and displayed his broad chest and lean hips to unfair advantage. She dragged her eyes away from him and put an extra couple of slices of bread in the toaster for herself.

'So, our young lady from the RTA yester-day—I gather she's had a good night and is looking better,' he said, watching her work.

'Yes—apparently. She's finished her trans-fusions and she's on saline now, and she seems comfortable.'

'She was lucky, you know. She had a stupid, gimmicky necklace on made of old beer cans cut up into triangles and bent onto a leather thong, and one of the triangles had sliced the edge of her carotid artery. If she hadn't had medical attention when she did, she would have bled to death within minutes, certainly before the paramedics got there.'

Julia threw tea bags into two mugs and poured boiling water over them. 'She was over the limit, you know. The police were in last night to talk to her. Her passenger's got spinal injuries, but nothing drastic. His kneecaps have both got starburst fractures, and his head's sore, but he was very lucky she wasn't going faster. Here, your tea. Help yourself to sugar.'

'I don't, thanks. He should have had his seat belt on, of course, then he probably wouldn't have been injured.'

'Whereas ironically her injury was probably caused by the seat belt cutting into her necklace,' Julia pointed out.

'No, it was caused by the stupid, dangerous necklace,' he corrected, plucking the toast from the toaster and dropping it onto the proffered plate. 'Looks good.'

'Butter, or marg?'

He grinned. 'I'll give you three guesses.'

She shook her head and slid the butter towards him along the worktop, together with a knife, and then spent the next few minutes trying not to stare at him as his even white teeth tore into the toast and the muscles in his jaw worked to chew it.

She scraped margarine on her toast and ate it fast, one eye on the time, and she was just swallowing the last bite when the door opened and Sally Kennedy put her head round.

'Ah, Julia, you're hiding in here. New admission—could you come? It's one for Owen Douglas.'

'Sure.'

She drained her tea and threw David a distracted smile. 'Sorry, I'm going to have to cut and run. Take your time—make more, if you want.'

'I'm fine. Thank you. You're a lifesaver.'

That smile again.

Blast.

She found herself spending the day wishing one of his patients would have a problem so she could call him back to the ward, but as luck would have it they were all fine.

Julia left the hospital on time, more or less, chastising herself for dawdling in the corridor just in case David was on his way to the ward, and then just to punish her God decided that her car was going to choose that afternoon to fail to start.

'Great,' she said, slamming her hands down on the steering-wheel and glaring at the bonnet. 'Marvellous.'

With no very real idea of what she might be looking for, she pulled the bonnet catch and spent several fruitless moments trying to get the safety catch off so she could raise it.

'Here,' a passing stranger said, and slid his hand under the edge, tweaked something and the bonnet came up into his hand. How intensely irritating!

'Thanks,' she said grudgingly, put the stay up to hold it and stuck her head into the engine bay. Not that she had any idea what she was looking at. She knew just enough to know that the engine hadn't been stolen, but beyond that she was stuffed.

A shadow fell over her line of sight, and she glanced up and straightened, bumping her head on the bonnet catch.

She yelped and clutched her head, and David tutted softly.

'You all right?'

'Oh, yeah,' she muttered ungraciously. 'My car won't start, goodness knows why, so I'm going to be late to fetch my daughter from school, and now just to improve things I've got a hole in my head.'

'That would be a no, then,' he said softly, and she laughed in spite of herself.

'In short.'

'Hmm.' He stood beside her and stared down at the engine, and hope dawned.

'I don't suppose you know anything about engines?' she asked him optimistically.

He chuckled. 'Not enough to fix them. I suppose you've got petrol?'

Julia nodded. 'Yes, I've got petrol, I filled it up at the weekend.'

'In which case,' he said, dropping the bonnet with a solid clunk, 'I suggest you get a taxi to your daughter's school and get a garage to come and look at it later. Do you belong to a motoring organisation?'

She shook her head. 'No—and there's no way I can afford a taxi.' Or a garage.

'In which case, can you drive an automatic?'

She stared at him blankly. 'An automatic? Yes, my father's got one, I've driven it a few times. Why?'

'Because you could take my car, get your daughter and go home, and I'll get my rescue service to come out and fix yours and then I'll drive it home for you and pick mine up.'

'But it's not your car! They won't do that.'

'It doesn't need to be mine. I just need to be driving it.'

He dangled his keys in front of her temptingly, and she hesitated.

'Don't you need it? Why aren't you working? And won't your wife or whatever mind if you're late home?'

'I've got the afternoon off. I was doing paperwork. I saw you from my window—and I don't have a wife, or a whatever, so she won't mind in the slightest. Come on, you can't be late for your daughter—unless your husband can pick her up?'

She shook her head. 'No—he's dead,' she said bluntly, not bothering to be subtle. 'Are you sure?'

'Of course. It's just over there—the silver BMW.'

'I'll crash it,' she muttered under her breath, and he winced and laughed.

'I'd rather you didn't,' he said mildly, propelling her gently in its direction. 'I've only had it a short while—not that it's new, but it still cost me enough, and I'm quite fond of it already.'

'What about insurance?'

'You're covered. Any driver over twenty five.'

She nodded. 'Thanks.'

He paused, his hands on the top of the door, just as she was about to drive it away. 'Your address would be useful.'

Julia felt a little rush of colour flood her cheeks. 'How silly. Sorry. Twenty-five Victoria Road. It's near the park.'

'I know it. I'll see you there.'

He shut the door firmly, and she eased out of the parking place and headed for the road, too absorbed in trying to avoid scraping his car against the barriers to worry about the fact that she'd just given him her address. It was only when she pulled up outside her house and took Katie in that she realised she'd broken one of her cardinal rules…

David watched her go, his face thoughtful.

So Julia was a widow with a daughter. That was tough. She couldn't be more than about twenty-seven or -eight, thirty at the outside. He wondered when her husband had died, and if she was over him or if she still cried for him in the small hours of the night.

He didn't know, but suddenly he wanted to find out. He'd spent the last few years moving around from one Special Registrar's post to another, completing his training, and now that he could finally settle down in one place, he was hoping in time to find a woman he could spend his life with.

And maybe, just maybe, that woman might be Julia Revell.

A slow smile nudged the corner of his mouth. He even had her address, thanks to the car. All he needed now was for the recovery people to come up trumps and fix it, and he'd be round there...

CHAPTER TWO

DAVID arrived at eight-thirty, but not in Julia's car.

'It needed a little part and he didn't have it, so he's taken it to the garage for repair,' he told her, not adding that he'd booked it in for a full service because it was clearly desperately in need of one.

Even so, her face fell. 'I wonder how much it'll cost? Oh, well, I have to have it. I can't survive without a car.'

Which was exactly what he'd thought, and why he'd phoned his father and borrowed the runabout they kept at the farm for his younger brothers and sisters when they were home from university.

'I won't ask,' his father had said wisely, and David had been unable to stop the little smile. Now he handed her the keys.

'It's a family runabout. You can have it till your car's ready.'

A tiny frown pleated her brow. 'Are you sure? That seems very generous. Won't someone need it?'

'It's not being used at the moment, they're all away at university still.'

'Oh. Well, if you're really sure...' She hesitated, then seemed to make a decision. 'Can I get you a coffee or something? Or supper? Have you eaten? You must have been hanging around for ages, I'm so sorry.'

He hadn't, in fact. The car had been dealt with by a quarter to six, and he'd been home and had had a meal with his parents and stalled until he'd thought her daughter might be in bed, but it wouldn't hurt to let her think he'd been hard done by.

· 'A coffee would be great,' he said with just enough enthusiasm. 'I've grabbed something to eat.'

He thought of the wonderful hotpot his mother had given him and waited for God to strike him down for dismissing it so casually, but it was in a good cause after all—and one his mother would be the first to further!

'Come in,' she said belatedly, stepping back and letting him into the hallway of her little Victorian terraced house.

He looked around at the stripped pine doors and pale walls, relieved by the careful place-ment of a few large, simple prints and colour-ful fabric hangings, and smiled. 'It's lovely. Have you been here long?'

'Three years. I moved here after Andrew died.'

He filed that information and followed her down the hall past the stairs towards the kitchen. A huge tabby cat was curled up in a sheepskin cat bed that hung from the radiator by the breakfast room door, and it yawned at him as he walked past.

He scratched its head and it purred and jumped out of the bed, trotting behind him into the kitchen.

'Arthur, you've been fed,' she told him, but the cat jumped up on the worktop beside her and nudged her with its big head.

'Horrible cat, get down,' she admonished, putting him on the floor, so he wound himself round David's ankles instead, sniffing them and checking out all the cats and dogs from the farm that had rubbed against his legs that evening.

Satisfied, it arched its back for a caress, and he bent and stroked it absently while he watched Julia moving around her little kitchen.

The units were dated, but the room was bright and cheerful and spotlessly clean and, like the rest of the house that he'd seen so far, it was welcoming.

Strange, then, that Julia seemed so edgy in a way, and so unlike the capable and efficient nurse he'd seen at work. Her body was like a coiled spring, the tension in her almost palpable. Did no one ever come here? She'd hesitated before inviting him in. Perhaps she was an intensely private person—or perhaps it was just because he was a man.

Instinctively he scooped up the cat and fussed it, and Julia seemed to relax slightly, as if he couldn't be threatening if he was an animal lover. To remove the threat still further he migrated to the breakfast room through the archway and sat down, thus shrinking himself—all the tricks he'd had to learn in paediatrics because of his size. He felt a twinge of guilt at manipulating her emotions, but told himself it was in a good cause. After all, he needed to get to know his colleagues.

She followed him, mugs in hand, and hesitated again. 'Are you all right here, or do you want to go through to the sitting room?'

He wanted to see the sitting room, or indeed anywhere else that would give him more clues to the person she was, but he forced himself to shrug. 'Wherever you're most comfortable,' he told her, figuring that the more relaxed she was, the more chance he'd have of getting to know her better.

She smiled softly. 'Here, then, as the cat's so comfy. He's not really allowed in the sitting room because he trashes the carpet and it's the only decent one in the house, so Katie and I spend a lot of time in here,' she told him, slipping into the chair opposite and settling down, her elbows on the table, her mug cradled between her slender hands.

Her fair hair slithered forwards and screened her face, and he had an almost irresistible urge to reach out and tuck it back behind her ear so he could see her expression better.

Instead he held onto his coffee-mug like a lifeline and concentrated on the silk-like softness of her hair, the tired droop of her shoulders and the little frown plucking at her forehead.

'My car,' she said after a moment. 'Which part did it need?'

David laughed and shrugged. 'I can't remember. Something to do with the ignition. Would it mean anything if I could remember?'

Her mouth kicked up in a wry smile and she shook her head, her hair slipping softly over her face again. She tucked it back out of the way, and he could see the smile still hovering around her lips. 'No. I wouldn't have a clue. I was just curious. It seems awful not to make the effort to understand somehow.'

'I gave up years ago when I moved on to cars with electronic ignition,' he said with a chuckle. 'It all got too complicated for me. I could understand carburettors and timing belts and stuff like that. The modern engine management systems give me the heaves.'

'So which garage is it at?' she asked, worrying her lip with her teeth.

'The one my father's always used. Don't worry, they're cheap and sensible.' And amenable to suggestion about rigging the bill, furthermore, but she didn't need to know that. He leant back in his chair, giving the cat more room to stretch out, and met her eyes over the table.

'This is a nice house,' he said softly. 'Friendly.'

Julia smiled again. 'We like it. The other one was modern and soulless—a detached ''executive''—' she wiggled her fingers in the air to make quotes '—house with an *en suite* bathroom and very little else to commend it. I hated it.'

Her smile had faded, and he pressed her gently for more information. 'Not your kind of thing, then?' he suggested, and she shook her head.

'It was Andrew's choice. I had to sell it when he died because—well, there was a problem with the insurance.' She hesitated. 'I couldn't afford to stay on even if I'd wanted to, but this came on the market, and it's quite handy for the hospital and the school, and, being near the park, it's nice in the summer. So I bought it. It's been a struggle but we're nearly through it now.'

Poor girl. 'It must have been tough, losing him,' he said, fishing again, and she rose to the bait like a charm.

'It was tough being married to him,' she said flatly. 'Losing him was the easy bit. Then...'

'Then?'

Julia looked at him blankly for a moment, as if she'd forgotten he was there, and then she shrugged. 'He had other debts. A card. They caught up with me just after we moved.'

'But surely you weren't responsible for that,' he said, puzzled, and her sad smile tore at his heart.

'It was a joint card,' she said. 'It was my own fault. I should have been more on the ball. Still, you live and learn and, as I said, it's been tough but it's nearly over now, and we'll survive.'

She tucked her hair behind her ear again, her lips pressing together as if she'd said too much, and sure enough she didn't go on.

Still, she'd said more than enough. Unable to help himself, David reached across the table and laid a hand over her wrist, quelling the anger that rose inside him. 'I'm sorry,' he said gently. 'I didn't mean to pry.' He was surprised to find he meant it. He'd obviously strayed into a very private part of her life, and one which, he guessed, she didn't share easily.

She flashed him a quicksilver smile, gone almost before he could register it, and he drained his coffee and stood up. Quit while you're winning, he told himself.

'Right, I'm off. I've got to go back over to my parents' tonight, because my house is without electricity at the moment. I shall be glad when it's done up and I can move in properly.'

'Where is it?' she asked, exhibiting a promising flicker of interest, and he reminded himself that she was probably only being polite.

'Just outside Audley—a village called Little Soham.'

'I know it,' she said, nodding. 'It's nice there.'

'It is. It's got a pub and a village shop and a post office, and a church and a village hall, and enough people to make it all viable. It also has a tumbledown little cottage with wonderful potential but in need of a huge cash injection—or more time than I'm going to be able to find. Probably both, in fact, but that's just my natural optimism leading me astray again.'

Her chuckle warmed him, and as she preceded him up the hall to the door he could smell the faint drift of perfume or soap or something.

She stopped suddenly and he bumped into her, her hair brushing his nose. Shampoo. That was what it was. She'd washed her hair, and it smelt of flowers and sunshine on a summer's day.

'Keys,' she said, turning to look up at him as he murmured an apology and moved back.

'I gave them to you.'

She patted her pocket and smiled, retrieving two sets of keys. 'So you did—and I forgot to give you yours back, didn't I? Sorry. Brain like a sieve. I can never find the ward keys either.' She paused, then looked up at him, her hand on the door catch. 'Thank you so much for all you've done this afternoon. I really am grateful.'

'My pleasure.' He looked down into her guileless smudge-grey eyes, and wondered if she'd run screaming if he gave in to his instincts and bent and kissed those moist, soft lips.

Probably. He smiled a little crookedly, took the keys of his BMW from her hand and walked down the path, his hand raised in farewell. Wise decision, he thought, because one kiss might not have been enough...

Julia shut the door and leant against the wall, her heart skittering under her ribs. For a crazy moment there she'd thought he was going to kiss her, and she'd felt herself start to sway towards him.

Thank goodness she'd caught herself in time! Imagine the embarrassment if she'd closed her eyes and waited like a lovesick fool for a kiss that hadn't come!

But she hadn't, thank goodness, because if she had and by a miracle he *had* kissed her, she would have had the problem of telling him she didn't get involved in relationships, and then having to work with him afterwards.

Too, too awkward.

Messy.

She shrugged away from the wall and ran upstairs to check on Katie. She was fast asleep, her little arm flung up on her pillow, her hair spread like a golden halo, her face innocent in sleep.

Julia reminded herself of all the reasons why she couldn't afford involvement with another man—and they began and ended with her small, vulnerable daughter. She was far too important to Julia to risk in any kind of emotional entanglement that stood the slightest chance of going wrong, and there were no guarantees with love.

She knew that to her cost, and so did Katie. Fatherless at two years old because of an act of mindless stupidity, and it had taken the best part of the next year to get her back on an even keel. Even now, nearly four years later, she was still a little clingy if Julia went out at night.

So she didn't, because nothing, and most particularly not herself, was more important than her daughter.

She'd do well to remember that.

'New admission with acute cholecystitis, woman of thirty-three, no previous history.'

'OK, Sally, thanks.' Julia perched a hip on the desk and tipped her head on one side. 'Have we got a bed?'

'Yes—Nick Sarazin's registrar just discharged two, so we've even got a spare!'

Julia grinned. 'Wonders will never cease. Right, let's go and get the bed ready.'

'You're too slow. The others have gone home and the beds have been done.'

'You're a love. I was only gone half an hour.'

'You ought to go for longer—just think what we could achieve!'

'I might leave you with the rota.'

Sally held up her hands, two index fingers crossed and held out towards her. 'Not the rota!' she begged theatrically. 'Anything but the rota!'

'It's the one thing I really hate about being ward sister,' Julia said with a grimace. 'I always seem to get it wrong.'

'Well, you know what they say. You can please some of the people some of the time...'

'Tell me about it. So, has David Armstrong seen his new patient?' she asked, going back to the original subject.

'I gather not. She's coming from a GP. She'll be here shortly— Ah, here's a trolley. This looks hopeful.'

It was, indeed, their patient, accompanied by her anxious husband, and Julia got her settled in a bed and started the ball rolling with a urine sample and a set of charts, a NIL BY MOUTH sign over the bed and the woman's first set of observations taken, while Julia soothed and studied her watchfully and took mental notes ready to report to David.

A firm, brisk tread behind her alerted her to his presence, and within the space of a heartbeat her skin was tingling, her breath had jammed in her throat and her legs felt like rubber.

Get a grip, girl, she scolded herself, but it was a fruitless task. Ever since she'd met him five days ago, her body had decided on its own response to his presence, and she might as well save her energy for more useful tasks—like dredging up what might pass for a smile.

Julia approached him, the smile fixed firmly in place, and quickly ran over the patient's present status.

'She's a bit shocky—seems to be in quite severe pain, her blood pressure's a little elevated, her respiration is light and fast, she's been vomiting and she seems very upset and distressed.'

He nodded. 'OK. Let's have a look at her, and then we'll start her on IV opiates to relieve the pain and see how she is then. I want her fluid balance done, please, and IV antibiotics. Have you got a tube down her?'

Julia shook her head. 'She only just arrived a few minutes ago. I've done a battery of urine tests. The results are written up.'

She handed him the notes, and he scanned them before approaching the patient and speaking gently to her and her husband. While he examined her she was very edgy and finally refused to allow him to touch her. It was a typical response to an acute attack of cholecystitis, and he covered her up again and turned to her husband.

'I don't think there's any doubt that she's got a handful of gallstones making a bid for freedom, but we'll run some tests once she's more comfortable and, depending on the results, I'll operate after the weekend. If the X-rays and tests show what I suspect, then we'll treat her conservatively over the weekend to let it resolve a little, and I'll operate on Monday morning. Pain relief first, though,' he went on, turning to Julia, 'and fluids, and I'll see her again later unless you're worried. OK?'

Julia nodded, avoiding those gorgeous piercing grey eyes, and after a moment he turned back to their patient. 'Right, Mrs James, Sister Revell is going to get you some pain relief, and then everything should start to feel a bit better, OK? We'll talk some more when you're more comfortable.'

The woman nodded slightly and moaned, and Julia quickly set up the intravenous line and gave her the first dose of painkiller. Within minutes she was feeling the benefit, and her breathing eased and she relaxed visibly onto the pillows.

'Better now?' Julia asked gently, and her patient nodded, a weak smile of relief touching her pale face.

'Yes, thanks. Oh, that was awful.'

'I'm sure. Right, we're going to slip a little soft tube down your nose and into your stomach to empty it so you don't have to keep being sick. That'll make you feel much better, too. Mr James, why don't you wait out in the corridor for a moment, and I'll call you back as soon as your wife's more comfortable?'

Sally helped her, and the procedure seemed to bring yet more relief to the beleaguered Mrs James. 'Oh, thanks, that's better,' she said weakly once her stomach had been drained. Her lids fluttered down and, after making her comfortable, Julia and Sally left her for a while to settle, her husband at her side again.

Two hours later David was back on the ward, striding towards Julia and doing silly things to her heart again.

'How's Mrs James?' he asked without preamble, but he made no move towards the woman.

'Settling. Quiet now, but still uncomfortable. Her obs are better.'

'Good. How's the car? Ready yet?'

She nodded. 'I rang them this morning—they said I could take the one you lent me over there and swap them, because they had to service it or something.'

'That's right.'

'I have no idea where the garage is, of course. Can you give me directions? I've only got the phone number.'

'I thought so.' He smiled, sending her off-kilter again. 'I thought I could do it for you this evening, if it helps. Take ours over and pick yours up.'

She chewed her lip doubtfully. 'I have to pay the bill,' she told him, but he shrugged it aside.

'I'll pay it for you—you can give me a cheque later.'

'If you're sure,' she said reluctantly. 'You seem to be going to a lot of trouble. I could do it myself quite easily.'

Except, of course, that Andrew's parents would be arriving to take Katie home with them for the weekend, and so she would have to be at home for that. Rats, she hated being beholden to anyone.

'I'll tell you what,' David went on. 'Take the BMW home, and I'll go straight from here with my parents' car and do the swap then run yours over to you. There'll be less messing around that way, and I'd have to take the run-about in for servicing anyway. Satisfy you?'

Julia smiled, relieved that it was sorted and that she'd get her own car back. She'd been having fits of guilt all week about driving his parents' car, and she'd been worrying about how she could do the swap that night. David's suggestion was the perfect solution—if only she didn't feel so guilty about accepting his help yet again.

And because she did, her guilt prompted a rash and silly suggestion.

'Andrew's parents are taking Katie for the weekend,' she told him. 'They'll pick her up at about six. Why don't you come for supper later when you bring the car back? Nothing exciting, just some pasta or something, just to say thank you.'

His eyes warmed with a smile. 'That would be really nice. What time?'

Julia shrugged. 'Seven?' To make sure that Andrew's parents were right out of the way and not likely to ask any awkward questions. Not that it was any of their business, and not that they would mind, but since there was nothing to know, really, they might as well not start to speculate. 'Is that all right? Or would you rather come later?'

'It's fine. I'll look forward to it. Now I suppose I really ought to go and see Mrs James.' He smiled at her a little crookedly, and she felt herself melting again.

'Do you want me to come?'

'Got time?'

'I can make time,' she said, thinking of all the things she still had to do before she went off duty, and how, if she was going to feed him tonight, she would have to find time to take Katie to the supermarket on the way home, so she couldn't afford to leave late.

They walked down the ward together to Mrs James, and found her asleep, her husband drowsing beside her.

'Mr James. How is she?' David asked him, and he blinked sleepily and straightened.

'Oh, Mr Armstrong. Sorry. She's better, thank God. We had an awful night last night before she'd let me call the doctor.'

'I'm sure.' David scanned the notes and nodded. 'She seems to be improving gradually. I think if we can just get her through this episode, I'll have a better chance of sorting her out on Monday without risk of infection. I don't really want to do it before then.'

'So she'll definitely need an operation, then?'

David nodded slowly at Mr James. 'I'm pretty sure she will, I'm sorry to say, but I'll do it with keyhole surgery if I possibly can, so she'll be up and about again within a couple of days and she should be home by Thursday next week, if all goes well. We'll see after the weekend. All right?'

Julia went with him up the ward, pausing to talk to one or two patients on the way, then he glanced at his watch and sighed. 'Back to the grind,' he said with a grin. 'I've got a clinic now. I'll see you later. Ah. Keys.'

Julia blinked. 'Oh—yes. Idiot me.' She went into her office and fished about in her bag for them. 'There might be one or two things in the car, I'm not sure.'

'I'll take them out and bring them back to you.' They swapped keys, and with a smile and a wave he was gone, leaving her with too much to do and a total lack of concentration to help her to do it…

The Revells were late, of course, but it was just as well because Julia had been held up in the supermarket after dithering over the supper menu.

Not that she had a great deal of choice, on her limited budget, but even though there was nothing between her and David Armstrong, somehow it still seemed important to do it *right,* and so she'd hovered and dithered in the salads, and debated the grossly expensive mange tout for three minutes before common sense had prevailed.

She still didn't know what her car was going to cost, after all, and she had to clear the rest of Andrew's debts. She'd chastised herself, bought ingredients for a simple lasagne and then had had to queue for five minutes, even in the supposedly quicker basket queue.

Then she'd spent another five minutes looking for her car in the car park before remembering that she'd had David's. By the time she'd got home she'd been flustered and panicking, and she'd snapped at Katie for dawdling over the packing of her little case and had then felt racked with guilt.

By the time Andrew's parents arrived, the lasagne was in the oven, the salad was washed and torn up and she and Katie were friends again.

'Hello, dear,' Annette Revell said, kissing Julia's cheek fondly. 'We thought you weren't here—we couldn't see your car.'

'No, it's in the garage. It broke down the other day. I'm getting it back later,' she explained, being frugal with the truth.

'Mummy's borrowed a car,' Katie piped up, dumping her in it, then added, 'from a friend,' just so there was no possibility of pretending it came from the garage.

'How kind,' Annette said distractedly, too preoccupied to take her up on it, thank goodness. 'Darling, we need to hurry,' she said to Katie. 'Grandad's parked on a yellow line—are you all ready?'

Katie nodded cheerfully, kissed her mother goodbye and left without a backward glance for another weekend of being spoiled rotten. Ah, well. Normally Julia would stress about it. Today she had too much else to worry about—like why on earth she'd invited a man to come to supper who did things to her blood pressure!

David parked Julia's car as near as he could to her house, then paused for a moment before going in. For some unaccountable reason he felt nervous, but it wasn't as if this was a date.

A thank you, she'd said, and she'd looked as if the invitation had been squeezed out of her by her conscience. If he'd had any decency, he'd have said no, but he really wanted to spend time with her.

Except that now he was here, he was suffering a little pang of what felt just like stage fright. With a wry chuckle he rammed his hand through his hair, dragged it down the back of his neck and sighed.

'Come on, Armstrong. It's just supper with a colleague. She doesn't have any interest in you. Chill.'

He scooped up the wine and the chocolates, hoped the Italian red would go with the pasta and that she hadn't changed the menu, and headed for the door. The bell rang, echoing through the house, and after a few moments he saw her through the glass running down the stairs.

'Hi,' she said breathlessly, pulling the door open. 'Sorry, the Revells were late taking Katie and I was a bit behind. Come in.'

Julia looked gorgeous, slightly flushed, her eyes wide, her hair flying like strands of silk, and his body leapt to attention. She might not have any interest in him, he thought wryly, but he sure as eggs was interested in her...

'So how often does she go to stay with them?' David asked.

Julia, her fork suspended on the way to her mouth, grimaced. 'Every three weeks. She loves it, but they spoil her dreadfully and I can't afford to— Which reminds me, what do I owe you for the car? I mustn't forget to pay.'

'Leaving the country?' he asked mildly, leaning back against the chair and smiling enigmatically.

'Of course not.' She ate the forkful, then looked at him again. 'So how much was it?'

'Thirty-two pounds,' he said. 'All bar a few pence.'

She sighed with relief. 'Right. I'll give you a cheque after supper.' She eyed his plate and pushed the lasagne dish towards him. 'Have some more. It doesn't keep.'

'I will. It's delicious.' He offered her a scoop, but she shook her head, content to watch him eat. More than content. Too much more. Darn, this had been a really bad idea!

She toyed with a little salad so she didn't sit and stare vacantly at him, and then finally he was finished and she whisked the plates away into the kitchen next door and brought back the pudding. 'Sorry, it's a cheat,' she said, serving up the little choux pastry balls filled with whipped cream and drizzled with chocolate sauce. 'I didn't have time to make profiteroles but these are quite fun and nearly the same. Cream?'

He smiled and took it, pouring on a generous slug and tucking in with enjoyment. 'They're nice,' he said, busy munching. 'Cheat or not, they work. I'm all for an easy life.'

They finished the little heap between them, scrapping over the last one and finally sharing it when he cut it in half with his spoon and fed it to her in a simple gesture that suddenly left her hot and cold all over and quivering inside.

Their eyes locked, and after an age he dragged his gaze away and ate the last half, licking a trace of cream from his lower lip with a kind of sensuous grace that made her mouth water.

'Coffee,' she said in a strangled voice, and almost fled to the kitchen.

As a retreat, it didn't work. David followed her and insisted on helping with the washing-up.

'It was supposed to be my treat, a thank you,' she protested, but he just smiled and lifted the dirty pans out of the sink and ran hot water into the bowl.

'I was properly brought up,' he told her, his eyes twinkling. 'Either you cook, or you wash up and put away. There were five of us. Chores were an inescapable part of life. So, I wash, or I dry and put away and you'll never find anything again. Which is it to be?'

Julia gave up in the face of his good-natured persistence, and laughed. 'You wash. I hate losing things.'

So they worked side by side at the sink, shoulder to shoulder, and she wondered what it would be like to work alongside him in Theatre as his scrub nurse, their bodies closely aligned and their minds focused in professional harmony.

Dangerous, she decided, and moved away a little, instantly missing the contact.

Not for long. Was it her, or him? One of them moved, just closing the gap a fraction so she could feel his warmth again and the light brush of his sweater against hers.

'So what are you doing over the weekend?' she asked to take her mind off his proximity.

'My house. The electrician's got the power on now, so I can make a bit of progress at last. It's hard to use the electric wallpaper stripper without power, for instance, and as sure as heck the kettle doesn't work!' He shot her a grin, and her legs went rubbery.

Oh, dear. Too dangerous. She moved away again, stacking the plates in the cupboard and giving him a wide berth for a moment. 'So how long will it be before you can live in it?' she asked.

'Oh, I can live in it. I've been living in it. It was only this week that was a problem. It's all a bit primitive, but it's fun in a rather pioneering sort of way.' He leant against the edge of the sink and looked at her, his head on one side. 'Fancy coming out tomorrow and seeing it for yourself? You could give me some advice. You've done some lovely things here, and I'd appreciate the help.'

Her mouth, in league with her traitorous heart and totally deaf to the screaming protest of her common sense, opened and accepted his invitation without missing a beat.

'Good,' he said with a smile. 'I tell you what, come for the afternoon and I'll cook for you—a trade off.'

'Only if you let me wash up,' she said, her mouth getting into the swing of it with terrifying ease.

'Done,' he said, and that was that. Oh, dear.

Before Julia could commit herself to any further folly, the dishes were finished and the coffee was made, and they went through to the sitting room. She'd lit the gas fire because it was chilly, and they pulled their chairs up and stretched their feet out to the flames and listened to the gentle hissing of the gas, and Julia found herself wishing it would never end.

It did, though, about an hour later, when their coffee was finished and her eyelids were drooping.

'You're tired,' he said softly. 'Why don't I go and let you get an early night?'

She felt a little pang of regret, but he was right.

'I feel too idle to move,' she told him, and he laughed and pulled her to her feet.

'Come on, lazybones. See me off and lock the door and go up to bed like a good girl.'

But she didn't want to be a good girl. The feel of David's warm hands around hers made her long to feel them elsewhere, touching her, holding her, caressing her...

She slipped her hands out of his and pushed her hair back from her face, tucking it behind her ears. 'You're a nag,' she told him lightly, and he chuckled.

'So I'm told. Never mind, you'll be grateful later when you don't wake up with a crick in your neck and cold feet.'

They went out into the hall, and as her hand reached out to turn on the light, he stilled it, catching her hand in his and easing her against his chest.

'Wait,' he murmured, his voice low, and then his lips brushed hers, just lightly, and her knees sagged so that she swayed against him. His arms came up round her, his mouth locked to hers, and out of nowhere came a heat so intense she thought her body would catch fire.

Just before the flames took hold he eased away, dropping one last feather-soft kiss on her lips before moving to the door.

'I'll pick you up tomorrow at two,' he said, and his voice was low and gruff and scraped over her nerve endings like rough silk.

Then he was gone, and she went back into the sitting room and curled up in his chair and relived the touch of his mouth against hers until the longing was so great she thought she'd weep with it.

She was seeing him again tomorrow, she thought, and even though her common sense told her it was too dangerous for her status quo, her heart soared with joy.

CHAPTER THREE

DAVID'S cottage was lovely. The roof was low, the walls red brick, and it was set back from the village green behind a little gate and a dense evergreen hedge that gave it privacy. There was no traffic to speak of, because the green was off the main route through the village, and it was peaceful and gloriously romantic.

That spooked Julia. After his kiss last night, she didn't need a romantic setting to make it even harder to keep their relationship in perspective!

Still, the interior did a little to dispel her fears. Far from romantic, it resembled a building site in parts, and she had to use her imagination to the full to picture how it would be when it was finished.

Not that it was cold or unwelcoming, but it was just, well, unfinished, to say the least. The front door opened straight into a large room

64

that ran the width of the cottage, with an in-glenook fireplace at one end and old oak beams that spanned the room, supporting the upper floor. Once done it would be lovely, but now it was bare except for an ancient sofa in front of the glowing woodburner and a lonely television sitting on the old brick floor in the corner.

David led her through into the kitchen behind it, which looked over the garden and across fields to the other side of the valley beyond. It was a very pretty view, and she could see why he'd fallen in love with it, but it was going to take years—or thousands of pounds—to put it right.

'I'm going to have a few hand-built pine kitchen units put in around that area,' he told her, indicating an L-shaped section of wall under the windows. 'Then over here I'll have a couple of dressers and things—very simple and unfitted, except for the bit with the sink and the washing machine and dishwasher, but they'll have to be built in so they don't show.'

'And a table?' she said, looking at the space in the middle and wondering if it was big enough. 'A table would be nice. Is there room?'

'Somewhere. I might have to find a little one or put it against the wall but, yes, a table in the kitchen is an absolute must! Come and see the garden while it's light. It's a mess, but it could be pretty.'

Julia looked at the tangled beds and over-grown shrubs with no real understanding. She'd never been much of a gardener—had never really had the time—and now she felt ignorant as he talked about hardy fuchsias and dividing clumps of perennials and the advan-tages of spring over autumn pruning.

He tipped his head on one side after a min-ute and looked at her apologetically. 'Sorry. You're not a gardener, are you? I must be bor-ing you to death.'

She laughed, anxious to dispel his worries. 'I wouldn't say I wasn't a gardener. To be hon-est, I don't know if I am or not. I've never really had the time to find out. My garden in Victoria Road is just a concrete yard and a tiny patch of rather tatty grass with a straggly shrub in the corner. Goodness knows what it is. I plant a few tubs in the spring to brighten it up and cut the grass when I remember.'

He chuckled. 'There's time to learn, if you want to. Your daughter might like it. We all spent hours in the garden with Mum, weeding and edging and hoeing the vegetables. Fruit picking was always the best bit. We never grumbled about having to do that, especially not the raspberries.'

She pictured a mischievous little boy with pink juice running down his chin, and laughed. 'I can imagine. No wonder you wanted to live in the country after a childhood like that. Did you help on the farm, driving tractors and things?'

'When we were older. At first we had to help with the animals. We had stock in those days, and there was always something to do, feeding calves or lambs or collecting eggs. We weren't allowed on the tractors until we were eight, and couldn't drive them till we were ten—our legs weren't long enough. It's all arable now, though, so it's easier. Wheat doesn't get you out of bed at four on a Sunday morning.'

'That would be easier,' she agreed, and his mouth quirked in that wonderful smile again.

'Absolutely. Come and see the rest.'

'The rest' turned out to be a neglected little orchard at the end, with a gnarled old apple tree in the corner with an ancient swing dangling from one branch. 'I'm going to plant daffodils and bluebells around here in clumps,' he told her, 'and have a wild bit—butterfly plants and so on. Do my bit for conservation.'

'Looks like nature's doing that already,' she said with a smile, and he chuckled.

'Let's go in and put the kettle on, and I'll show you the upstairs. It's pretty much as it was. I haven't got round to trashing it yet, but the bathroom's next on the menu. That'll be fun, having the water off. Oh, well.'

'Pioneering spirit, you said.'

David grimaced good-naturedly and shut the back door behind them. 'So I did. Come on up.'

He flicked the button on the kettle in passing, and led Julia back into the main room of the cottage and through a little door at the far end by the fire. It opened to reveal stairs climbing steeply to the next floor, and he led her up them, warning her to mind her head, although she was nothing like as tall as him so it was easier.

'I'm having an extension if the plans are passed—just a single room downstairs and one up, with a proper staircase onto this landing, because getting furniture up these is a nightmare.'

'I can imagine,' she said, looking round as they reached the top. 'Gosh, it's a huge landing.'

'Well, not really. Technically it's a small bedroom,' he told her with a grin, 'and the other one is through there. I'm going to divide this up to make a bathroom, and the bedroom in here...' he ducked through the doorway '...will be split into two again as it used to be. Then the new room at the back overlooking the fields will have its own bathroom as well.'

She looked around and nodded, and wondered if he was good with his hands. He had to be, she decided, because there was a lot of talk of 'I'm going to do this' and 'I'll put this here', as if he intended to do the work himself.

Besides, he was a surgeon, so it wasn't hard to imagine that he'd be practical.

They went back down the twisty staircase to the kitchen, and while he made a pot of tea she sat in the comfy carver and studied him appreciatively.

Odd, how she'd thought he was bulky when she'd first seen him. He wasn't at all, she considered thoughtfully, just broad-shouldered, with a deep chest. At somewhere around six feet tall there was a lot of him, but he was fit and muscled, and in those old jeans that snuggled his lean hips he looked good enough to eat.

'Hungry?' he asked, and she wondered guiltily if her eyes had given her away.

'Pardon?' Lord, did she really sound so breathless?

'I asked if you were hungry. I've got some of my mother's fruit cake. It's good—not too rich, so you don't feel over-indulged, but tasty enough to be a real treat.'

'Sounds lovely,' she said, dredging up a smile that hopefully wasn't too inane and wondering if her thoughts were as clearly written on her face as she imagined them to be.

Apparently not, or, if they were, he was ignoring them. They took their tea and cake through to the sitting room, such as it was, because it was chilly in the kitchen even with the portable gas stove, and David had lit the woodburner in the sitting room in the morning, so it was lovely and cosy.

They sat together on the two-seater sofa in front of the fire because there was nowhere else, and he handed her the tray while he pulled up a bright plastic toolbox to put it on.

'I like your coffee-table,' she teased, and he grinned.

'Good, isn't it? You don't see many like that.'

'Certainly not, although I have to say it's a little colourful for my taste.'

The smile lurked around his mouth as he lay back into the corner of the sofa, his mug balanced on his belt buckle, and sighed contentedly. 'I'm glad you're here. I should be stripping wallpaper.'

'Don't let me stop you,' she advised, her mouth twitching, and he closed his eyes and chuckled.

'Oh, I think I should. Ignoring a guest would be too rude to contemplate.'

'I could help you, when we've finished our tea,' she suggested a moment later. 'I'm good at it—lots of practice. There were six layers in my bedroom.'

He cracked an eye open and peered at her. 'Really?'

'Really. I counted them.'

He sat up. 'No, I mean, really, you'd help me?'

Julia gave a wry laugh. 'Why not? I've got nothing else to do that won't keep, and I hate being in the house when Katie's away. It seems so empty and desolate.'

'So we could look on it as a little therapy for you so I don't have to feel guilty, is that right?'

She chuckled. 'If it makes you feel better. Actually, I just enjoy it. Or I could cook if you'd rather.'

'And get out of the washing-up? Not a chance. No, we'll have our tea and then we'll turn the radio on and strip to music.'

He was only teasing, but she felt her cheeks heat. 'In your dreams,' she retorted, trying not to remember her dreams of the night before or how empty and alone they'd left her feeling.

He pulled a wry face and grinned. 'Worth a try. We'll take some wallpaper off, then, if you insist.'

'I do,' she said firmly, but as he smiled that understanding smile at her, she found she wished she didn't.

Monday morning seemed to take for ever to arrive. He'd dropped her home at ten thirty on Saturday, after a wonderful casserole that she had a sneaking suspicion had come from his mother, and she'd dreamed of him again and woken restless and unsettled. Sunday had been a day of catching up with jobs—the laundry, the cleaning—and then Katie had come home, full of all the things she'd done and all the places she'd been, and Julia had felt inadequate as usual because she didn't have any money to spend on the child in such frivolous ways.

She could, of course, have asked his parents for help with paying off the credit-card debt that Andrew had run up, but her pride forbade her. Julia told herself he'd been her husband at the time, although they'd been separated, and she should have taken steps to close the account. It had, after all, been a joint card, and thus she had still had responsibility for the debts on it when he'd died.

She'd just never thought about it. He'd changed the address, so the statements hadn't come to her, and she'd totally forgotten the card existed.

More fool her. It had been a mistake she wouldn't make again, but in the meantime Katie was being spoilt by his parents and Julia was having to deal with the fallout.

So it was with relief for several reasons that she went into work on Monday morning, and her first job after taking report was to prep Mrs James for surgery. The test results had come back showing a handful of stones obstructing her gall bladder, and she was to have keyhole surgery first thing that morning to remove them.

'Are you sure he'll be able to see well enough through a tiny hole?' Mrs James asked Julia as she explained the procedure again. 'I mean, are you sure it's safe?'

'Yes, I'm sure. He'll fill up the inside of your abdomen with carbon dioxide gas to separate all the bits and pieces, and then he'll use a thing called a laparoscope to see inside you, and the surgical instruments will be pushed through little holes in your side and tummy and he'll guide them using the laparoscope. The gas helps to hold everything apart so he can see more easily.'

'And afterwards I'll feel much better much quicker, is that right?'

'That's right. You won't feel nearly the amount of pain you would with a conventional open operation, and your recovery will be much, much quicker. You should be home in a couple of days if all goes according to plan.'

'And if it doesn't?'

Julia perched on the side of the bed. 'In the unlikely event that he wants a closer look or it's worse than he'd thought, you'll have the conventional operation and you'll be in hospital a week or so longer—but don't bank on having a holiday at our expense,' she added with a reassuring smile. 'I gather he's very good.'

'I'm delighted to hear it,' a deep voice said from behind her, and she turned quickly, her hand flying up to her chest.

'You gave me such a fright,' she said with a laugh, and stood up. 'I was just assuring Mrs James that the likelihood of her staying here longer than a couple of days more is slight.'

David nodded, the warmth in his eyes changing to professional concern and greeting as he turned to Mrs James and smiled at her.

'Morning. How's my patient?'

'Still very sore, but much better, thank you, Doctor.'

'Good. Well, hopefully by tonight you'll be much more comfortable. I'm planning to do you first, so you'll get a head start post-op and you won't have to hang around now. OK? And I'll come and see you later.'

He turned and gave Julia his professional smile. 'I wonder if we might have a word?'

'Of course.'

Julia walked up the ward with him, wondering what he wanted, but he didn't keep her in suspense long. 'I've got a problem,' he told her quietly. 'The plumber's starting this week, and when we're on take I need to be nearer than I am at my parents'. Is there a room I can use if I reach a critical stage and the water's cut off?'

'Sure, there's a room on the ward and another in the doctors' residence,' she said, simultaneously relieved and disappointed that his question was so mundane. She had hoped for some reference to their weekend.

'Unless, of course, you want to put me up for the odd night?'

Her eyes widened, but then she caught the teasing glint in his and pursed her lips. 'You're dreaming again,' she told him, and he gave a silent huff of laughter.

'No comment,' he said in low voice, and there was a hint of something in there that made her wonder if he, too, was being plagued by sleepless nights and wild dreams.

'You need to make sure your SHO isn't using the room on the night you need it,' she reminded him, refusing to let her mind be sidetracked.

'No. He probably wouldn't appreciate having to sleep with me,' he said with a chuckle, and Julia caught herself just before she said something stupid that would give her clean away.

'Anything else?' she said brightly to cover her almost-lapse, but he shook his head.

'No, nothing, just the information about the room.'

'While I think about it,' she said, remembering her drive to work that morning, 'thank you so much for getting my car fixed last week. That part must have been going wrong for ages, you know, because it's running like a charm. I don't think it's ever run as sweetly as it is now. I thought it needed servicing really badly, but it must have just been that one bit, which is a real relief because just now I don't have the money to pay for a major service.'

Something flickered in his eyes and was gone. 'Good,' he said heartily. 'I'm glad it's done the trick.' He glanced at his watch. 'Lord, is that the time? I'd better get up to Theatre. I'll see you later.' He paused for a second, then shook his head.

'What?'

'I was going to suggest lunch, but I doubt if I'll be finished in Theatre before two, and you go at three. Never mind. We'll do it another time.'

She agreed without thinking, and then as he walked away she shook her head slowly. Supper here, lunch there, then a real date, then—wham! Involvement.

Unless she kept it all very neutral and didn't let him close to her. She could enjoy his company, couldn't she? Just go out with him from time to time if he asked her, nothing heavy, no commitment, just two friends.

Then she remembered the kisses…

*   *   *

Mrs James had her keyhole surgery as planned, and went home on Wednesday morning, delighted to be feeling so much better and clutching her jar of gallstones as a trophy.

'I'll put them on the mantelpiece when the in-laws come,' she said mischievously, and Julia chuckled.

'Highly ornamental. Or you could make a candle and suspend them in it like those pretty ones with leaves and things all round the sides, and use it for a table centrepiece on Christmas Day!'

'It might put the others off, but at least I'll get to enjoy lunch,' she said with a grin. 'Better out than in.' Her smile faded, and she took Julia's hand in both of hers. 'Thank you so much for all you've done. I know that to you it was just a simple operation, but to go from what I felt like on Friday morning to how I feel now is nothing short of a miracle for me, and I'm really, really grateful. Thank you.'

She leant forwards and kissed Julia's cheek, hugging her slightly before letting go and laughing a little breathlessly. 'Oh, dear, I'm going to cry in a minute,' she said, and blinked away a sheen of tears.

Julia waved her off, sorry to see her go. She'd been uncomplaining and cheerful, unlike some of the others. Old Mrs Bailey was groaning at the moment, but Julia knew the moment her visitors arrived she'd be sitting up in bed as perky as a parrot.

'My dear, this sheet's creased again,' Mrs Bailey said petulantly as Julia paused beside her. 'It's really most uncomfortable. It's the mattress, I'm sure. Couldn't you find me a better one?'

'It's the plastic covers,' Julia explained. 'The sheets slide around on them. I'm sorry, they're all the same. Let me straighten the sheet for you.'

She whisked the curtains round the bed, turned back the covers and straightened the offending sheet with a swift tug, tucking it firmly back under the mattress. 'Better?' she asked, and Mrs Bailey nodded grudgingly.

'I shall be glad to get home to my own bed,' she said, and Julia could sympathise with that. There was nothing like your own bed, and a plastic-covered mattress in a public ward was certainly nothing like it.

She looked at her patient more closely, and saw the weary lines around her eyes. 'Are you sleeping all right?' she asked, and the woman shook her head.

'No. Of course not. They all cough and fidget and call out, and, besides, I can't get comfortable because I'm in pain.'

Julia could well believe it. She'd had a very tricky resection of her stomach and duodenum following years of supposed indigestion that had turned out to be chronic ulceration and inflammation, and her post-op recovery had been slower than expected. Despite Mrs Bailey's difficult nature, she felt her sympathy aroused. Her sympathy, and her instinct.

'I'll get Mr Armstrong to look at you when he's next on the ward—perhaps he can write you up for something that will make you feel better,' she said gently.

Mrs Bailey sank back against the pillows and closed her eyes. 'Oh, I hope so. I really am very tired of it, and it does seem to be getting worse.'

Julia wondered if the cheerful act with the visitors was just that, an act, and if Mrs Bailey really was suffering more than she was letting on. She paged David, and asked him to call in on the ward when he was passing.

'I was just on my way up anyway,' he said. 'I wanted to check something in some notes before my next case. I'll see you in a minute.'

He appeared shortly, looking somehow even more appealing than ever in blue scrubs, and he smiled that smile and nearly dissolved her bones.

'Right, what's the matter?' he asked, and she told him that she felt Mrs Bailey wasn't progressing and just looked a bit off colour.

'I don't know, it's probably nothing, but my instincts tell me things aren't right. Her bowel sounds haven't come back yet, and she's looking peaky. I don't know—she's just not getting better fast enough.'

He nodded. 'OK. I'll buy that. I'm a great believer in instinct, especially coming from an experienced professional like you.'

It wasn't flattery, it was delivered as a statement of fact, and it made her glow all over.

He went with her and looked at Mrs Bailey, examining her carefully and checking her charts. Because he'd taken over from her consultant when he'd left, he hadn't performed the operation, but she was now in his care and he was clearly going to take Julia seriously.

'I think I'd like a scan of that,' he said. 'I wonder if there's a little abscess forming? We'll do some blood tests as well. If you've got an infection brewing you will be feeling rough. Sister Revell, perhaps we could discuss the tests I'd like done?'

David led Julia up the ward, his fingers rubbing his chin thoughtfully. 'I don't like the look of her,' he said quietly. 'I think you're right, there's something going on in there—I reckon I'm going to have to open her up again. Let's not jump the gun, though. I'd like a thorough look through her notes before I commit myself, and an MRI scan and the bloods. Can you sort that out for me? I'm on call overnight, so I'll be here. If necessary we can take her up to Theatre this evening.'

'I'll get it all organised now—the results should be back by late this afternoon if you're lucky.'

'You mean if I lean hard on the lab?'

She smiled. 'Something like that.'

'I'll bear it in mind. What are you doing at lunchtime?'

She cocked an eyebrow at him. 'Chivvying the lab for you?'

'Wrong. Having lunch with me before I start my afternoon list. Got time?'

She thought of her resolve to keep him out of her daughter's life, but lunch was hardly a threat to Katie's stability and, besides, she had to eat.

'I'll make time,' she promised, and the warm glow in his eyes filled her with anticipation. Good grief, she thought, we're only talking about lunch here, but her heart was singing for the rest of the morning.

She met him in the larger of the two canteens, but before they could get their meal his pager bleeped. He scanned the message, rolled his eyes and dropped it back in his pocket. 'No peace for the wicked. I have to go to A and E. I'm sorry.'

'David?'

He paused in the act of turning away. 'Yes?'

'Tonight,' she said, without allowing herself to think. 'What are you doing all evening, if you aren't needed?'

He shrugged. 'Just hanging around.'

'Want to hang around at my place? I could give you supper—if you want to. It's only five minutes from the hospital in the evening.'

His eyes softened and he smiled slightly. 'Thank you,' he said in a low voice. 'That would be wonderful. What time?'

She laughed. 'You're on take. Whenever you can get away. I'll do a casserole and feed you when you get there. Any time after seven-thirty.'

'After Katie's in bed.'

She refused to feel guilty about that. 'Yes,' she confirmed, and he nodded, his smile wry.

'OK. After seven-thirty it is.'

In fact it was nearer nine, because he had three cases tacked onto the end of his afternoon list and he had only just finished them, he explained when he arrived.

'You look bushed,' she told him, and he grinned tiredly.

'There's a surprise. I'm also starving. I haven't eaten since breakfast.'

'Good. Come on through.'

He followed her down to the kitchen, shedding his coat onto the back of a chair on the way, and then stood behind her, his arms round her waist and his head on her shoulder while she dished up.

'Smells good. You do, too,' he murmured, and she felt shivers run down her spine.

'You smell of hibitane,' she told him bluntly, and he chuckled and let her go, moving away to give her room to move.

Perversely she didn't want that much room, but she could hardly tell him she found the smell of hibitane curiously exciting and would he come back, please, and hold her again!

Julia handed him a plate groaning with mashed potatoes and a steaming chicken casserole, and scooped up her plate and cutlery.

'In here, or in the sitting room on your knees?' she asked.

Arthur was sleeping peacefully in his sling on the radiator, and David looked bushed. 'Sitting room?' she said, making the decision for him, and he nodded.

'Absolutely,' he said. 'Then I don't have to move after I finish.'

He didn't. Not only did he not move, he fell asleep within minutes, and she took the plate carefully off his lap and let him sleep. She probably could have felt offended, but he'd been working hard and who knew what the night might hold?

In fact, he only dozed for a few minutes, then he woke and stretched and smiled apologetically. 'Sorry about that,' he said softly, and she felt a well of tenderness inside her.

'Don't be, you needed it. Coffee?'

He shook his head. 'No. Don't move. Just come here.'

So she went to him, and sat beside him on the sofa, her head on his chest and his arm around her, and he sighed with contentment and pressed his lips to her hair. 'This is nice,' he murmured, and she had to agree. It was something she could grow very used to, and if she could only summon up the resolve, she'd fight it.

But she couldn't, so she didn't, and they sat there for over an hour before his bleep squawked and he had to return to the hospital.

'All good things come to an end,' he said as he shrugged into his coat. 'Thank you for this evening.'

'My pleasure. Shall I wake you in the morning?'

David laughed. 'If by a miracle I should happen to be asleep. Tea would be nice.'

'Don't push your luck.'

He kissed her, a tender, lingering kiss that held a wealth of promise, and Julia closed the door behind him and went back into the sitting room, watching him cross the road and drive away with a wave of his hand and a flash of headlights.

The house felt extraordinarily empty without him.

CHAPTER FOUR

JULIA tapped gently on the door of the duty room and opened it a crack. It was quiet, the silence broken only by the soft sound of David's breathing. She slipped inside and closed the door behind her, setting the tea down on his bedside table and perching on the edge of the bed.

'Hey, sleepyhead,' she said softly, and he blinked and yawned and grinned sheepishly.

'Hi. Sorry. I meant to be up. What time is it?'

'Ten to seven. I managed to get Katie up a little earlier today. She was excited because they're casting the nativity play today and she wants to be Mary, so she couldn't wait to get to school. How was your night?'

He groaned. 'Grim, and I have to go back to Theatre now with Mrs Bailey, but there's a problem. We're a scrub nurse short. I don't suppose you can lay your hands on anyone with Theatre experience who could do it, do you?'

She thought rapidly. Sally Kennedy was on with her that morning, and while she was quite capable of running the ward, she hadn't worked in Theatre for years. Whereas Julia herself...

'I could do it,' she offered. 'If it's only the one case.'

'It is. Would you?'

She thought of standing hip to hip with David, watching him work, and a little bubble of anticipation rose in her chest. 'Sure,' she said, trying to sound nonchalant. 'When?'

'Soon as you like. I think she's prepped.'

'I don't know. I haven't seen Angie yet. I'd better go and check it's OK before you get excited.'

'Good idea. Is that a cup of tea for me?' he asked hopefully, peering at the bedside table, and she nodded. 'Great.' And without hesitation he lifted himself up on one elbow, reached his arm out of the sheets and picked up the cup, giving her a tantalising display of his bare chest and shoulders.

Oh, lord. Her heart backed up into her throat, her blood pressure rocketed and if anyone had asked her, she probably couldn't have remembered her name.

'I'll go and see Angie,' she mumbled, and headed for sanity.

Not for long, though. Sally appeared and confirmed that she was happy to run the ward for an hour or so, and then David emerged from his room fully dressed a few minutes after she'd woken him and filled her in with the results of the scan.

'It looks like a piece of the stomach wall has died following the resection—maybe the blood vessels were disrupted by the operation and a bit was left without adequate supply. Whatever, we need to open her up and find out, or she'll just continue to deteriorate. She's been on antibiotics since last night, and hopefully it should be straightforward.'

'Hopefully,' Julia commented, eyeing his shoulders in the crisp white shirt and trying not to remember what they'd looked like just a short while ago, the bare skin sleek and warm and tempting. Too tempting. They looked good enough in the shirt to test the resolve of a nun. Anything less was just downright unfair. She forced herself to concentrate on Mrs Bailey.

'Have you explained to her?' she asked, and he nodded.

'She's not surprised. She said she's been feeling worse and worse for the past three days or so.'

'Why didn't she say anything? She just got grumpy with the staff, and all the time she must have been feeling dreadful. Maybe she just didn't register how serious it might have been—perhaps she thought it was just part of the recovery process, like itching of the wound and that kind of thing.'

'Who knows? Anyway, I'm going up to Theatre. Want me to send someone down for her now?'

'You could. I'll have a chat to her and come and scrub.'

And so she went and told Mrs Bailey she was assisting in the operation, and the elderly woman took her hand and squeezed it and said she was glad.

'I trust you, dear,' she said simply. 'You can tell me all about it later.'

'I will,' Julia promised, and then she went up to Theatre, scrubbed and changed and came out of the dressing room to find David sitting with a cup of coffee in his hands, waiting for their patient.

'Hi, there,' he said, and she felt suddenly conscious of the blue pyjamas and whether she looked hippy in them. She was bound to. *Everyone* looked hippy in them—well, everyone except him, of course, because he hardly had any hips, just shoulders and a deep chest and powerful arms.

Oh, heck.

'How's Mrs Bailey?'

'Fine. Wants a blow-by-blow account of the op later.'

He grinned. 'I'll let you do that—especially if we don't find anything and we've opened her up for nothing,' he said, but in the event they found a small black section of stomach wall which had withered and died without a blood supply, as David had suspected, and he removed it, patched and repaired the hole and then closed the wound with neat stitches, leaving healthy pink tissue that would heal quickly and put Mrs Bailey on the road to recovery.

He was a joy to watch, and for a few minutes Julia forgot about the feel of his hip against hers and concentrated on watching the precise and careful movements of his hands as he inserted the fine sutures.

'I've got some mending at home. I think I'll let you have it,' she teased, and his eyes creased over the mask.

'In your dreams,' he murmured, and straightened, flexing his shoulders and rolling his head. 'Right, she'll do. Thank you, everybody.'

They left her with the anaesthetic staff and went into the changing area, and Julia's side felt cold without him next to her. How odd, she thought, because normally she didn't like to be too close to people.

Well, men, anyway, and yet David, for all he was all man and hugely attractive to her, seemed in no way a threat. Instead, being that close to him just seemed...right.

Very right. Worryingly so.

A little late to do anything about it, she realised she'd allowed him to become important to her. Not only that, she'd maybe allowed herself to become important to him, and that was unfair, because there was no way anything permanent would come of their relationship, or even anything more serious than what they were already indulging in.

But what were they indulging in? she wondered. A little light flirtation? Friendship? Nothing overtly sexual—nothing that smacked of an affair about to be embarked upon. There were no suggestive remarks, no forbidden touches, no stolen kisses—just friendship, and the occasional goodnight kiss that didn't even get mildly out of hand.

Maybe she was blowing it up out of all proportion. Maybe it was only her, and he was unmoved.

'Thank God that's over,' he said now, stripping off the top of the blue scrubs, and with one last longing glance at his powerful back and shoulders, she headed for the changing room.

He might be unmoved, but she wasn't. If she'd had the slightest hope that it would work, she would have had a cold shower, but she had a horrible sneaking suspicion that it would take more than a simple dousing in icy water to subdue her feelings for David Armstrong...

'So will I get better now?'

'Oh, yes. I'm glad I had the chance to assist him. He's a very careful, thoughtful surgeon. He'd be a good builder—measure twice, cut once, you know the sort of thing.'

Mrs Bailey smiled faintly and nodded. 'Good. I shall look forward to feeling more my old self, then.'

Julia settled her down comfortably on her pillows and left her to rest. She'd been too groggy yesterday for much of a conversation about her surgery, but today she'd had questions that Julia had been able to answer, and now she seemed content to relax and allow herself to get better.

It was a shame she'd had the setback, but these things sometimes happened. Julia found herself wondering if it would have happened if David had performed the initial operation, and wondered just how biased her answer was.

Very, probably! Oh, dear. She really was losing her perspective on this man, and just to mess her up worse, she could hear his voice in the office. It sounded as if he was on the phone, and he appeared beside her a moment later, a smile warming those astonishing eyes.

'Hi, there. I just borrowed your phone to speak to a GP. I hope you don't mind.'

'Of course I don't mind. It's hardly my phone.'

His smile widened. 'Some people are very territorial about their ward phones.'

'I have better things to worry about,' she said primly, and he chuckled.

'Of course. How's Mrs Bailey?'

'Happy. I told her you were wonderful.'

'Naturally. What else would you tell her?'

'The truth?' she suggested, and then spoilt it by laughing. 'I told her you'd make a good builder.'

He rolled his eyes and laughed. 'Is that supposed to inspire confidence?'

'Yes—her husband was a builder. It's a concept she understands. Talking of builders, how's the house?'

'Oh, coming on. I should have a bathroom by the weekend. Want to come and see?'

She pulled a face. 'I'd love to, but I've got Katie. I'm going to need to spoil her a bit because she didn't get the part of Mary in the nativity play. She's got to be a lamb, and she's disgusted. Maybe another time.'

David's eyes met hers, troubled and a little saddened. 'Am I ever to be allowed to meet your daughter?' he asked gently.

She looked away. 'I don't want her getting caught in the cross-fire,' she said, all humour banished. 'I don't think it's a good idea.'

'Nor do I, but what cross-fire, exactly? I don't see us fighting, and we aren't involved in an intimate relationship that's going to cause questions. I really don't see the problem. I'm a friend, Julia. I'd like to be more, but for now I'm just a friend. Surely she's allowed to meet your friends?'

A flashing light caught her eye, and she latched onto it like a drowning man to a straw. 'I have to go, someone needs me.'

'No, they need someone. Not necessarily you. Julia, think about it. I'll talk to you later.'

And he walked away, leaving Julia staring after him and wondering if, indeed, he really was only a friend and if she and Katie could spend time with him without harm coming to her daughter. The weekends were often long, and she had more and more trouble finding cheap, fun things to do.

Maybe visiting David's cottage and going for a walk in the country might be rather fun, she thought, allowing herself to be tempted. After all, with Katie there he was hardly likely to do anything to threaten the status quo—even if at times she might rather want him to, against all common sense.

The flashing light called her still and, putting aside her personal thoughts and feelings, she went back to work.

Just friends, he'd promised her, and he spent the whole of Saturday morning telling himself that as he worked on the cottage. She and Katie were coming over that afternoon, and he was cleaning it up and trying to make it look less like a bombsite and more like a home.

Fruitless task. He stopped himself picking a bunch of greenery out of the hedge and sticking it in a milk bottle on the kitchen window-sill. Dear me, he thought, you're losing it.

Instead he concentrated on picking up the scattered tools so that Katie wouldn't fall over them and hurt herself, and making sure he had an adequate supply of his mother's biscuits and lots of juice and milk and so on for her to drink.

At a quarter past one, just as he was clearing away the last dustsheet from the sitting room, there was a tap on the door. He opened it, dropping the sheet behind it, to find Julia there, an apologetic smile on her face and a tiny, bright-eyed little girl with blonde curls fizzing round her head staring up at him in obvious excitement.

'Sorry we're early,' Julia began, but Katie cut her off.

''S my fault,' she said. 'I wanted to see your house. Mummy said it was re-e-eally pretty and got a big garden with a swing, and I wanted to come now!'

Julia's smile was apologetic. 'She's been nagging since seven this morning. I hope we aren't too early.'

'Of course not,' he said, unable to help the smile. 'Come in. I was going to change, but you've caught me. You'll have to take me as you find me, I'm afraid.'

A pale wash of colour ran over her skin, interestingly, and David stored that little snippet for later consumption. Suppressing his smile, he led them both into the kitchen and offered them refreshments.

'Juice, please,' Katie said politely, and perched on the edge of a chair, sipping her orange and nibbling a biscuit while he made tea. He noticed her eyes kept sliding to the back door, but she didn't say anything. He was impressed. Julia might have had to bring her up alone, but she'd done a good job, from what he'd seen so far.

'Right, while the tea cools, what would we all like to do?' he asked, and her eyes lit up.

'I want to see the swing,' she said, and Julia was just opening her mouth when he got there first.

'I think that can be arranged. Julia, shall we take our tea up the garden with us?'

'It's freezing,' she pointed out, but he just smiled.

'We can wear coats.'

So they put on their coats, and while Katie swung gently back and forth on the swing with its creaky branch and rusty chains, Julia and David stood nearby in a pool of sunlight and drank their tea and watched her.

'She's enjoying herself,' Julia said softly. 'Thank you so much for suggesting it. The weekends are getting difficult.'

'Because of her grandparents?'

'Partly,' she confessed, unwilling to blame them too much. After all, it wasn't their fault they had money and wanted to spend it on their grandchild. 'Partly because we've done all the obvious things a million times.'

'Well, I'm only too happy to be of service,' he said with a wry smile. 'It's not a lot to ask, letting the kid have a go on the swing.'

'Can we go for a walk round here?' she asked, and he shrugged.

'I don't know. I'm not sure of any of the walks, I haven't had time to try them yet. We could go to my parents'. She'd love it there. She could help pick up the eggs and things, and play with the dogs and cats. There are some puppies at the moment.'

'Puppies?' Julia said, weakening visibly, and he pushed the slight advantage ruthlessly.

'They'll be going soon. They've all got homes but Mum won't let them go so close to Christmas, so they're only there until just afterwards. They need children to play with, to help them socialise.'

She was struggling. 'What sort?' she asked, a tiny thread of yearning in her voice, and he played his ace.

'Golden retrievers. Mum breeds them. They're lovely—like little woolly bears. They're cute,' he added, and watched her crumple.

'Well…maybe for a short while,' she conceded, and David had to restrain himself forcibly so he didn't punch the air.

'We'd better make a move, then. It takes twenty minutes to get there from here, and it's cold and dark so early at the moment.'

She nodded, and called to Katie. 'Would you like to go and see a farm, and some puppies?' she asked, and the child skidded off the swing and ran over, bright eyes shining, curls bouncing.

'Puppies?' she squeaked excitedly. 'Real ones?'

He chuckled and hunkered down. 'Absolutely real. They belong to my parents. Want to go?'

She nodded so fast it was a wonder her head didn't fall off, and they moved her booster seat from Julia's car into the back of the BMW and set off, and all the way there Katie bombarded David with questions about the puppies and the farm until his head was reeling.

Then they pulled up outside, and she skipped up the path to the back door beside him, little face shining up at him, and he lost his heart.

'Stay for supper.'

Julia hesitated, unwilling to overstay their welcome, and Mrs Armstrong smiled understandingly.

'You're more than welcome,' she said firmly. 'The house is just too quiet these days with the youngsters away at university and David moving into his own home. I can't get used to cooking for two and I always overdo it. We've got a big casserole—Jeremy would be delighted if you'd help to eat it up so he doesn't have to have it for days running.'

Julia looked at David for help, but he just shrugged. 'I'll take you home if you like, but I'm coming back for supper. I can't resist Mum's casseroles and she knows it. It's up to you.'

'Please, can we stay?' Katie asked pleadingly from her position in the puppies' playpen in the corner of the kitchen. She had three of them asleep on her lap, sprawled across her like fat furry butterballs, and three more resting against her legs. Extracting her was going to be worse than pulling teeth, Julia realised, and gave in.

'All right—but just for supper. Then we have to go home.'

'Can we take a puppy home?'

She sighed inwardly. She'd known this had been coming since the moment David had first said the word. Fortunately Mrs Armstrong had an answer, because she couldn't bear to have to say no to yet another thing her child had set her heart on.

'I'm afraid they all belong to people already,' she said kindly, pausing beside the playpen to look down at Katie with a smile. 'But they will need someone to play with them and cuddle them from time to time until they can go to their new homes after Christmas. If your mother doesn't mind, you'd be very welcome to come over and do that until they go— and by then we might have some kittens. One of the farm cats is looking suspiciously fat. And in the spring there'll be a couple of lambs to play with and lots of baby chicks.'

Katie's eyes were like saucers, and Julia felt panic rising in her chest. So much for keeping Katie and David apart! His mother was sucking them in relentlessly, giving her daughter a million and one things to look forward to that all depended on her relationship with David— a relationship she wasn't even sure she had or could cope with.

She looked at him in desperation for help, but he was watching Katie and his mother and smiling indulgently. So, no help there, then.

Supper was wonderful, of course, not only because the food was delicious but because they were both made to feel so welcome. Katie was never excluded from the conversation, and Julia only realised later quite how much of herself she'd revealed during the course of the meal.

They were so easy to talk to, though, and the glass of mulled wine beforehand by the drawing-room fire might have had something to do with it. Whatever the reason, she found she'd told them a little of their lives since Andrew had died, all in very neutral terms, of course, because Katie had been there and Julia made it a habit not to discuss Andrew in a derogatory way, but they weren't stupid, and she'd seen the understanding in their eyes.

'What are you doing for Christmas?' Mrs Armstrong asked as they cleared the table. Katie was back in the puppy pen, Mr Armstrong was walking the dogs and David was busy with the washing-up.

Julia shrugged. 'Nothing much. We'll spend it quietly at home. We'll probably go for a walk in the park.'

'What about family?'

She shook her head. 'My parents live in Lancashire, and my brother and sister-in-law and their children are going to them. It's a long way to go just for two days, and I'm working the morning of Christmas Eve and again the day after Boxing Day, so I can't really squeeze it in this year. Katie will spend the weekend before with Andrew's parents, having their own little Christmas while I'm on duty. They'll spoil her to bits—it'll be her real Christmas, I suspect.'

'You could come here,' Mrs Armstrong said softly. 'There's always room, and I know

David would love to have you. All the others will be back, so it'll be a bit manic, but we'll still have the puppies and David's sister's children will be here for Katie to play with as well. Why don't you think about it?'

She could picture it—warm and colourful and loud and loving and the most wonderful fun. She ached for it, and a huge lump formed in her throat. 'I couldn't,' she said, the words almost torn from her, but she could feel them being sucked in deeper and deeper, and the desperate longing to be part of it terrified her.

'Think about it,' Mrs Armstrong said again, and Julia nodded blindly.

'We ought to be going soon,' she said, putting the plates down beside David on the draining board.

'Ten minutes,' he promised, and she nodded and picked up a cloth and wiped the cutlery absently and worried about how she could refuse their invitation for Christmas without hurting all their feelings. All three of them had been so kind to her and Katie that day, and she wondered what David had said to his parents about her, if anything.

They hadn't expressed any surprise or untoward interest in her, just an easy acceptance of her as a friend of his, but Julia was afraid they would start expecting more. After all, he was thirty-two, still single, and most men would be seriously thinking of settling down by then, if not before.

Was David? Was that why he was interested in her?

Because, if it was, it really wasn't fair to him to allow him to spend time with her, because she had no intention of allowing their relationship to develop into anything serious and it was only right that he should know that from the outset.

All she had to do was tell him so.

She was quiet on the way home. David watched her out of the corner of his eye, and the child sleeping in the back of the car, and wondered what was on her mind.

He had a feeling he knew. She'd withdrawn from him since supper—well, since his mother had issued the invitation to come for Christmas. She'd done that while he'd been in the kitchen, but he'd heard her, and his heart had sunk.

Too much too soon, he'd thought, and it seemed he might have been right. Could he undo the damage, though?

'Don't let my mother crowd you,' he said now, softly so as not to disturb Katie. 'She's always throwing the door of the house open to anyone who strays within reach. She means well, but sometimes people feel a little over-whelmed.'

'She's lovely,' Julia replied in a low voice. 'Really welcoming. She makes Christmas sound very tempting, but I think it would be better if we don't come.'

'Keeping Katie out of our relationship?' he murmured, and she flashed him a quick, star-tled glance.

'We don't really have a relationship,' she reminded him, and he sighed inwardly.

'We could.'

'No.'

'We could be very discreet. Katie need never know, if you didn't want her to.'

He glanced across at her and surprised a look of yearning on her face. Ruthlessly he pressed his advantage, and slid a hand across onto her lap, twining their fingers together. 'Julia?'

Her fingers clung to his for a moment, then his hand was placed carefully back in his own lap, and she retreated. 'No.'

'I won't give up. I'm a persistent man,' he told her gently.

She didn't answer, just turned her head away and looked out over the moonlit countryside as he navigated the roads back to Little Soham. He pulled up outside the cottage and turned to her again.

'Do you want me to drive you home and pick you up in the morning to fetch your car? It seems such a shame to wake Katie and put her into a cold car. And besides,' he said, trying to inject a little humour, 'you still haven't seen my new bathroom.'

She sat motionless for a moment, then her shoulders seemed to droop and she turned back to him, a resigned smile on her face. 'I haven't, have I? That was rude of me.'

'I agree. I think you should remedy it.'

She nodded. 'OK.'

'So shall I take you home?'

'Please.'

David tried not to smile too victoriously, but he felt as if he'd won a major concession.

And he'd see her again tomorrow.

Life was suddenly looking up.

She must have been mad. Fancy agreeing to let him bring her home last night so that she had to see him again today! And after all she'd said about them not having a relationship!

What an idiot. It would give him all sorts of false hope and encouragement, and make him even more persistent.

Julia yanked open her sweater drawer and looked in despair at the miserable collection of old knitwear. She had nothing decent to wear. He'd seen her only respectable sweater about three times now, and he must be heartily sick of it, but it was too cold to go without and, anyway, her blouses and shirts weren't much better.

And then she realised what she was doing, and slammed the drawer shut in disgust. 'You're a fool, Julia Revell,' she told herself crossly. 'You don't want David, so why are you trying to make him want you?'

Because I do *want him, and I want him to want me.*

It was a sobering thought.

CHAPTER FIVE

OF COURSE, the day didn't start and end with the bathroom inspection. They went for a walk, and then because Katie begged and pleaded they went back to the farm and played with the puppies again, and as Katie seemed happy Julia and David took the dogs and went for a ramble in the woods behind the farm.

'I wasn't doing this,' she told him with as much firmness as she could muster, and he smiled that smile that did incredible things to those gorgeous eyes and crumbled her resolve even further.

'Of course not,' he said soothingly, and took her hand and tucked it into his pocket, their fingers entwined, and the warmth of his hand spread through her entire body and threatened to melt it.

She would have taken her hand back, but she was too weak. It felt good snuggled up with his in the warmth of his jacket, and she could feel the hard pressure of his hipbone against the back of it, shifting rhythmically with his stride. Lean, hard male, focused on her, she thought, and it was giddily intoxicating.

They climbed uphill a little, and then came out through a break in the trees and looked back down towards the farm. They could see the smoke curling from the chimney, and the edge of the roof, but nothing else for miles except a church spire in the distance.

'It's beautiful here,' she said wistfully. 'What a wonderful place to be brought up.'

'It was. I love it. That's why I came back.'

David stood behind her, his arms round her waist and his head resting lightly on her shoulder, and she felt the soft puff of his breath against her cheek as he nuzzled her ear.

'You smell good,' he murmured, and Julia felt his lips move softly over her jaw and down the side of her throat. She tipped her head instinctively to allow him access, and she felt the hot, moist trail of his tongue across her throat, and the icy coolness of his breath as he blew softly on the damp skin, bringing her whole body singing to attention.

'Come here,' he murmured, and without releasing her he turned her into his arms and kissed her.

It was a long, slow, drugging kiss, nothing hasty or hurried, just a leisurely mating of their mouths, a gentle exploration that left her weak and wanting more. Much more.

More than was good for her.

She eased away, looking up at him with eyes that must have held a host of conflicting messages. 'No,' she said, but she didn't sound convinced even to her own ears.

'Yes,' he murmured back, and drew her closer, claiming her mouth again.

She pushed him away, more firmly this time, and he laughed softly and let her go.

'Spoilsport,' he murmured, but he didn't push it, for which she was hugely grateful because she was already missing the contact with his body and for two pins would have gone straight back into his arms and given him anything he asked for.

That was scary.

He took her hand in his again and led her back down to the house. Katie was still in the playpen with the puppies, but it was time for their food so David lifted her out and the puppies were fed and left to sleep.

'One of them weed on me,' Katie announced without any great concern.

'I'm not surprised,' Julia told her. 'Are you very wet?'

She shook her head. 'No. It was only a tiny wee. Here.'

She showed her mother the wet patch on her leg, the size of a large coin, and then told her all about the puppies—that they didn't have names yet, because the people who were going to have them would give them names and so they had to be just called 'puppy' until then, and how they were just five and a half weeks old now and would be going to their new homes at seven weeks, just after Christmas.

'Can we come every day and play with them?' she asked, and Julia stifled the urge to say yes and shook her head.

'No, darling, of course not. Mrs Armstrong doesn't want us here in the way all the time and, anyway, you're at school in the day and I'm at work. There isn't time.'

'Next weekend, then,' she pleaded, but Julia pointed out that next weekend she would be with Granny and Grandpa Revell.

'But I won't see them again, then, because it's nearly Christmas and they're going!' she said, and burst into tears.

Julia looked helplessly at David, who just shrugged. 'You can come every day,' he said under his breath.

'No.'

'Or at least once or twice, in the evening.'

'I don't know the way.'

'I'll bring you.'

'No.'

'Please!' Katie sobbed, and Julia felt as if she'd been put through the wringer.

'Why don't you stay for lunch and let her play with them again after their sleep?' Mrs Armstrong suggested practically, but that was almost worse, because it just seemed as if they were moving in wholesale.

'Did you have any other plans?' David asked, and she shook her head.

'No. Not really. I need to do something with the washing and ironing, and my vacuum cleaner thinks it's been made redundant, but apart from that...'

'Sounds like a good reason to play hookey,' David said with an easy grin.

'What about you?' she asked. 'I've hijacked your day again. You wanted to get on with the cottage.'

'Did I?' he said mildly. 'I'm sure it won't catch fire if I turn my back on it for another day.'

'You could leave Katie here after lunch and go and get on, the two of you, and pick her up later,' Mrs Armstrong suggested. 'I've got nothing else to do today apart from the chickens, and your father's out for the day at a vintage farm fair in Norfolk, so I'd be quite happy with the company.'

Julia could feel herself wavering. On the one hand she had the temptation of David and a happy child, on the other hand she had Katie miserable and the housework to do.

No contest.

'Are you sure?' she asked, despising her weakness and yet tingling at the thought of spending more time with him.

'Absolutely. Let's have a quick lunch and you can go and get on. Ham sandwiches all right?'

'Your mother's very kind.'

'She's just a mum. She misses the others—says it feels odd without children underfoot. That's why she breeds the puppies—it satisfies her maternal instincts. So, what are you going to do for the rest of the afternoon? Do you want to go and do your housework, or do you want to come and dabble in DIY with me?'

'What are you going to be doing?' she asked, not at all drawn to her ironing board.

'Bits of this and that. The bathroom's all plumbed in but I need to fix the bath panel and stick on the tiles and paint the walls.'

'Do you have the tiles?'

He nodded. 'Yes. Why? Fancy sticking them on?'

'I could. I'm quite good at tiling.'

His grin was infectious. 'Excellent, because I seem to have squiffy eyes. I can never get them on straight.'

So Julia spent the afternoon sitting on the side of his bath with her feet in the tub, sticking white tiles all over the walls around the bath and up towards the ceiling at the tap end because he had a shower mixer, while he painted the walls around her.

'There,' she said in satisfaction, sticking the last one in place. 'You can grout them—I hate that job.'

He chuckled. 'You and me both, but at least they're straight. Thanks.' He put the roller in the tray and looked down at her from the top of the stepladder. 'Tea break?'

She looked at her watch. 'Shouldn't we be going back for Katie? It'll be suppertime in an hour.'

'Exactly. If we time it just right, we'll get fed, too.'

'David, that's awful,' she said with a shocked little laugh. 'We can't just eat there all weekend!'

'Why not?' He came down the ladder and tapped the tip of her nose with a blunt forefinger. 'Don't worry. Mum loves company. Anyway, she's expecting us.'

She stared after him as he left the room and headed for the stairs. 'Excuse me?' she said to his retreating back. 'What do you mean, she's expecting us?'

He turned back at the top of the stairs and threw her a smile. 'I said we'd be back then. Come on, wash that adhesive off your hands and come and have some tea. You worry too much.'

Did she? She didn't think so. She was beginning to feel she hadn't worried anything like enough nearly soon enough, because David and his family seemed to have wormed themselves firmly into their lives while she wasn't looking.

Julia washed her hands thoughtfully and went downstairs to find him pouring boiling water into two mugs. 'Cake?' he offered, but she shook her head.

'No. David, this is ridiculous. We're there all the time—'

'Are you bored there?'

'Of course not.'

'Is Katie suffering? Are we doing anything to hurt her?'

'No, of course not—'

'Well, then. Stop worrying. Here's your tea. Going to change your mind and have cake? It's my mother's date and walnut.'

And yet again, for what seemed like the hundredth time in the past two days, she weakened.

'Morning.'

Julia's heart fluttered betrayingly at the sound of David's voice, and she lifted her eyes from the paperwork and feasted them on his face. 'Morning. You're here bright and early.'

'I've got a tricky case. I wanted to go through the notes again.'

'Mr Burrows?'

He nodded. 'How is he? Good night?'

'Seems so. I was just sorting out these discharge papers and then going to see him. I think he's a bit apprehensive.'

David eased a hip onto the corner of her desk and smiled wryly. 'Not surprising. He's got very little to look forward to in the immediate future, and I'm just hoping I'm going to be able to give him some good news after the op, but I'm not optimistic. He's had his symptoms too long, and cancer of the bowel doesn't respond well to neglect. Have you got the notes handy?'

'Sure.'

She stood up and pulled the notes out of the trolley and handed them to him. 'Want a cup of tea? I've got a few minutes before I go and do the drugs, and we've got plenty of staff on this morning for a change.'

'That would be lovely,' he said, lifting his head from the notes for just long enough to flash her a smile.

She made two mugs and took them back into her office, and found him ensconced in the chair beside the radiator, the notes open on his lap. He was staring at X-rays on the light box, and he looked thoughtful.

'Working out how to tackle it?' she said, and he nodded.

'It's going to be tricky. I won't know until I get in there just how bad it is, but I think I'm going to have to remove the first section of his colon and reattach the end of the ileum to the top. Hopefully he won't need a colostomy, but I'll know more when I get in there.'

He slapped the notes shut, dropped them on her desk and picked up his tea with a smile. 'Thanks. I'm ready for this. I'll go and talk to him in a moment.'

He stretched his legs out, feet crossed at the ankle, and dropped his head back against the wall with a sigh. 'So when are you coming to grout my tiles?' he asked with his eyes shut, and she laughed.

'Never. I told you, I don't do grouting. It's a horrible job. It always takes me ages and I never manage to get all the grout off the surface of the tiles, so they always look cloudy and patchy.'

'I think you're just making excuses,' he said lazily, and buried his nose in his mug. 'I think anyone who took pride in their work would want to finish the job.'

'Is that right?' she said, going back to her paperwork and pretending to ignore him.

David placed a large, flat hand in the middle of the form she was filling in, and she looked up into his laughing eyes and felt herself start to smile.

'Did you want something?'

'My grouting.'

'Beggars can't be choosers.'

'I'll swap you.'

'Swap what?'

'I'll take you out for dinner next weekend, while Katie's with her grandparents.'

Julia laughed. 'You must hate it even worse than I do,' she said, and he chuckled.

'You can have no idea. So that's a deal, then.'

'No.'

'What?'

'You heard.' She stopped pretending to work and looked up at him again. 'David, we don't have a relationship,' she said quietly.

For a few seconds he was silent, searching her eyes, then he gave a gentle sigh. 'I disagree. I think we do have a relationship—and

I think it would be a tragedy not to explore it and extend it.' He straightened up, taking his hand off the form, and looked down at her with tender and understanding eyes.

'Give us a chance, Julia. I know you're running scared, but we could have something really special here. I feel it, and I'm sure you do, too, or you wouldn't have spent so much time with me already.'

He glanced at his watch and sighed again. 'I have to go and see Mr Burrows, then I have to start my list. I'll see you later—and think about what I said.'

'You just want your grouting done,' she said, trying to lighten the tone, but she sounded nervous and panicky, and he just smiled.

'We'll talk about that later.'

He went out and closed the door softly, and she stared blankly at the form on her desk and wondered if she dared allow him to talk her into this, or if it was just madness.

Her heart was skittering against her ribs, her breath was jamming in her throat and she could feel panic rising like a tide to swamp her.

He's not Andrew, she told herself, but even so she was afraid. She'd been vulnerable before, and she'd been badly hurt. Did she dare risk it again?

'Mummy, can David and his mummy and daddy come to my nativity play? I want them to see me being a lamb.'

'Oh, darling, I don't know if they can,' Julia said, trying not to dash her daughter's hopes too cruelly. 'David's very busy at work, and his parents have all the puppies and hens and things to look after. What about Granny and Grandpa Revell?'

'I don't want them. I want David. Can you ask him? Please, Mummy!'

She hesitated. 'Well, yes, I can ask, but don't get too excited. When is it?'

'Tomorrow.'

'Tomorrow!' Julia exclaimed, horrified. 'I didn't realise it was so soon! Oh, darling. They might be busy. Anyway, how many people can you take?'

'Don't know—I got a letter. Hang on.' Katie rummaged in her little schoolbag and came out with a crumpled form. Julia smoothed it on the kitchen table and scanned through it.

'You can take two people, it says here.'

'You and David,' she said promptly.

Oh, lord, Julia thought. I can't sit there with him and watch my daughter in a nativity play like real parents! What will the teachers think? What about the other mothers?

'Please, ring him,' Katie said, handing her the phone.

She stared blankly at the instrument. 'I don't have his number,' she said, and realised it was true.

'Is he at the hospital? Ring him at the hospital, Mummy. Please—I really want him to come.'

Oh, lord. She looked at her watch. He might still be there.

'I'll try,' she said, and dialled the number and asked them to page him.

He came on the line a moment later, sounding crisp and efficient.

'David? It's Julia. I'm sorry to trouble you at work, but I don't have your home number, and Katie wanted to ask you something.'

'Look, I'm tied up just now. Can I pop in on my way home?'

He sounded harassed, and it flustered her into agreeing. 'Sure. Sorry. It's not important.'

'Yes, it is!' Katie protested, and she heard him chuckle.

'Don't worry. I'll see you later—about six.'

Which, of course, was just when their supper would be ready. Julie looked at the little cottage pie in the oven and wondered if it would stretch to feed him as well. Not a chance. Oh, blast. Still, she didn't want to invite him. She was busy telling him they didn't have a relationship—she couldn't then invite him for supper with the next breath! She peeled carrots and trimmed sprouts—just enough for the two of them—and by the time he arrived the table was laid for two and the supper was ready.

She opened the door and stood there in the hall, deliberately not inviting him in. 'I'm sorry to drag you out of your way,' she began, 'but Katie wanted to ask you to come to her school nativity play. Please, feel free to say no.'

He laughed softly and leant against the doorframe. 'I wouldn't dream of disappointing the child. Just tell me when and where.'

Just then Katie realised he was there and came flying down the stairs, curls bouncing, and skidded up to him with a sparkling smile.

'It's my nativity play tomorrow night at school—can you come? I can have two people, and Mummy's one of them, and I want you to be the other one. Please, say you can—please, please, *please!*'

'Tomorrow?' he said, hunkering down and pulling out his diary. 'Let's see—Tuesday. OK. What time?'

'Six-thirty,' Julia said. 'At the school on Northgate Avenue, but parking's a bit hit and miss.'

'How will you get there?' David asked her.

'I'll walk from here with her, a little early. You could park here and walk with us, but it might mean hanging around for a while, or you could meet us there—if you really can spare the time?'

He looked up at her, his eyes laughing. 'Wild horses wouldn't keep me away,' he told her firmly, and any hope she'd harboured that he'd back out fizzled and died on the spot.

'Have you come for supper?' Katie asked, taking him by the hand and dragging him into the hall.

'No—I haven't been invited,' he said, looking at Julia with teasing eyes over Katie's head.

She felt colour sweep her cheeks, carried on the tide of a little rush of guilt. 'Do you have plans for tonight?' she asked, and he shook his head.

Her heart was in her mouth, but she forced herself to smile at him. 'Would you like to spend the evening with us? It's nothing special, but you're welcome to join us, if you'd like. I can do some extra vegetables.'

David searched her eyes, seeing probably far too much, and then he smiled. 'You're trying to get out of the grouting,' he said softly, and she laughed a little breathlessly.

'You guessed. Well?'

'I'll stay—whatever the reason,' he said quietly. 'Thank you.'

'It's more or less ready. I just need to do the veg,' she said, dragging her eyes from his and telling her heart to behave. 'Come on through. Katie, go and wash your hands ready for supper, darling.' And I'll just spend the next twenty-four hours wondering how to introduce this gorgeous hunk to the other mothers without inspiring a whole host of searching questions!

The gorgeous hunk in question followed her down the hall to the kitchen, hanging his coat on the banisters on the way past and propping himself up against the worktop while she opened a tin of sweetcorn and heated it in the microwave. There was an apple pie lurking in the back of the freezer, and she gave that a whirl in the microwave, too, and put it into the oven to warm and crisp as she dished up, all under David's watchful eye. 'So why the change of heart?' he asked softly, and she dolloped shepherd's pie on the worktop instead of the plate.

'Change of heart?' she said, scraping it up and putting it onto her plate. 'What makes you think I've had a change of heart?'

'The fact that I'm in here having supper and not talking to you through the letterbox? The fact that earlier today you weren't having anything to do with me, and tonight you ask me to your daughter's nativity play?'

'No,' she corrected. 'Katie asked you to her nativity play. It was her idea—and it's just the sort of thing I was worried about. But it's too late, because you're coming now and I'm just going to have to deal with the fallout.'

'Fallout?'

'Fallout—as in, who was that man with you on Tuesday night?'

'Ah. That sort of fallout.'

'Mmm. Got any good ideas?'

He shrugged. 'Tell them I'm a friend of the family. It's not a lie.'

It was a definite thought, and a huge improvement on any of the things she'd come up with. Anyway, it was impossible to continue the conversation because Katie came bouncing in, hands still damp, and turned them palms up for inspection.

'Lovely. Go and sit down, and take David with you and lay another place. I'll bring the supper in a minute.'

Katie towed him away, and Julia sank back against the wall and sighed. Maybe letting him join them for supper had been a mistake, but it would have been impossible to retract Katie's invitation without being unpardonably rude.

Damn.

Oh, well, the damage, if there was any, was done. Julia finished dishing up, took the plates through and put them down and drew up her chair.

'I'm afraid there isn't much,' she said, patting hers down to spread it so it didn't look so small, and he looked from plate to plate and smiled slightly.

'It looks a lot better than whatever I would have had at home. Thank you,' he said quietly, and he ate his small portion without a word of complaint.

'I'm still hungry. What's for pudding?' Katie asked, and Julia produced the now warmed apple pie, put a dollop of ice cream on each slice and watched them wolf it down.

'More?' she asked, and two sets of hungry eyes met hers.

'If you can spare it.'

'Of course I can spare it,' she said. 'Anything to get out of the grouting.' David laughed.

'What's grouting?' Katie asked.

'The white stuff in between all the tiles. You have to squash it in with a rubber thing called a squeegee, and your mother hates doing it,' David explained.

'It's boring—and, anyway, they aren't my tiles.'

'Whose tiles are they, then?' Katie asked, looking puzzled, so Julia explained about finishing off the tiling in the bathroom at the cottage.

'I'll do it!' Katie offered enthusiastically. 'I like squidgy things.'

'I think it's a bit too difficult for you, my darling,' Julia told her, 'and, anyway, you're too busy with your play and everything.'

'I'm a lamb,' she told David, looking disgusted. 'It's a stupid part. I wanted to be Mary, but they said I was too little, and one of the big girls got it, but I wanted it.'

'Maybe next year,' David said reasonably. 'You'll be bigger then—and, anyway, being a lamb is very important. Each part is important. Without the lambs the shepherds wouldn't have a job, and without the shepherds who would have followed the star and visited the baby Jesus?'

Katie thought about that for a moment, then perked up. 'I'm the smallest lamb,' she told him. 'Just so you know.'

'I'll look out for you.'

'Right, young lady, bathtime and then bed,' Julia said, and Katie pulled a face, but she wasn't letting her get away with it just because David was there. Maybe he'd take the hint and go, Julia thought, but he just stretched out at the table and relaxed.

'I won't be long,' she told him, and by the time she came down he'd washed up and dried all the dishes and left them stacked on the side. The kettle had boiled, mugs were on standby beside it and he was reading a magazine at the table in the breakfast room.

'Good grief,' she said faintly. 'Ever thought of taking a job as an au pair?'

He chuckled and came up behind her, sliding his arms round her and nuzzling her neck. It was something she could get rather used to, she thought, shifting her head slightly to give him access.

'Tea or coffee?' she asked dreamily, but he turned her into his arms and kissed her, and she forgot that she was supposed to be keeping their relationship cool and kissed him right back.

After a moment he lifted his head and looked down at her with eyes that blazed with heat. 'Wow. Where did that come from?' he murmured, and moved away from her fractionally. 'Just remind me that your daughter's in the house and we can't do this,' he added, and retreated to the next room and the safety of the magazine.

'Um—tea or coffee?' she asked again, and he gave a strangled laugh.

'I don't care. Just put a hefty sedative in it.'

She bit her lip to stop the smile, and took the tea through to the breakfast room, putting it down on the table in front of him with a hand that shook slightly. 'Tea,' she said. 'Unfortunately I'm right out of sedatives. I'll pick some up next time I go shopping.'

He chuckled, but his eyes were still heated and there was a tautness to his jaw that hadn't been there before. He didn't say anything, though, just picked up the tea and sipped it thoughtfully in silence.

It wasn't a companionable silence. It was charged with emotion, with need recognised but not fulfilled, and Julia wanted nothing more than to put her tea down and go into his arms and finish what they'd started.

Instead she changed the subject. 'How's Mr Burrows?' she asked, and he arched a disbelieving brow.

'You want to talk about Mr Burrows? OK. Well, he's not wonderful. The tumour was more widespread than the scan suggested, and it had tracked to the lymph glands, so the prognosis is pretty dismal, I'm afraid. I've done all I can do for now, and I'm discharging him to the oncologist once he's healed from the surgery. All they can do is keep him comfortable, I'm afraid, and slow the progression maybe.'

'What a shame.'

'It is. He's a nice man. Very stoic. That's the trouble. He should have pressed the panic button a bit sooner.'

'How long do you think he's got?' Julia asked, knowing full well that any answer would be wildly inaccurate but just seeking to extend the conversation a little longer—anything rather than go back to that charged silence!

David gave her a level look that spoke volumes. 'You know better than to ask me that,' he said with a wry smile. 'Three months? A year? Who can tell?'

'Does he know?'

He shook his head. 'No. He was too ill yesterday after his surgery to discuss it. I want to get him a day or so down the line before I broach it.'

He put his mug down, looking at her with those clear rainwashed eyes, and she felt as if he could see deep into the innermost recesses of her soul. She looked away, but he was undeterred.

'Julia.'

She drank her tea, ignoring him, but he reached across the table and took the mug out of her hands, and tilted her chin up so she was facing him.

'Look at me,' he said softly, and she met those wonderful eyes and felt sick with anticipation. 'We have to talk about this,' he went on, his voice gentle but implacable. 'There's something simmering just under the surface, and we both know it, but you keep trying to deny its existence, and I want to know why.'

Because of Andrew.

She moved away, standing up and going back into the kitchen, fiddling with the kettle. He followed her, but he didn't touch her or crowd her, just stood nearby, watching her silently.

'My husband left us,' she began, her voice flat as she remembered that awful day. 'Katie was eighteen months old. I'd moved down here with him the year before, leaving my family and friends, because he wanted to be near his parents.

'I made a few friends, but not many. He was a bit possessive, and he used to flirt with my friends—it was embarrassing. We had the odd dinner party that ended in disaster because he couldn't manage to restrain his hands and the husbands got upset. He blamed it on me—said I'd gone off sex since Katie and what was a man to do? Anyway, one day we had a blazing row because I'd been out for coffee with a friend and he'd come home from work expecting to find me there, and I wasn't.'

She paused, remembering his temper and frustration, and shook her head. 'He waited for me, and went berserk when we got back. He told me I was a waste of space and he didn't want any more to do with me, and he wanted a divorce. He packed a bag and left, and came back at the weekend and took all the rest of his things. He was living with his parents, and they took his side, of course, while I had no one.'

'Why didn't you go home to your parents and friends?' he asked, and she laughed a hollow little laugh.

'Because I was married. I'd made vows that I believed in, and I kept hoping he'd come back. I thought it was my fault, and it was years before I realised that it was him and not me that had had the problem.'

David shook his head slowly, his eyes full of understanding. 'So what happened then?'

'He died. That winter, just before Christmas, he had an accident one night, going home drunk from an office party, and managed to kill himself. Fortunately he had nobody in the car with him, and he hit a tree. Then I found out he'd cancelled the endowment policies and the mortgage wasn't cleared, so I had to sell the house and look for somewhere with the small amount of equity that was left. Then, just after I bought this house with the money I managed to scrape up, the credit card company caught up with me and gave me a bill for ten thousand pounds that he'd run up on a joint card.'

David muttered something derogatory under his breath, and she gave a tiny laugh. 'Oh, yes. He really was a piece of work. So now I don't trust anyone but myself, and I've always sworn I'll never give anyone else the power to hurt us or threaten our home in any way. So...I'm sorry, but that's why.'

'So even in death, he's still got the power to ruin your life.'

Julia tilted her chin. 'My life isn't ruined. I have my daughter, and I love her more than you can imagine. I have a good job, and a lovely home. I have everything I need.'

'Not quite,' he said softly. 'You're still denying yourself the right to an adult relationship.'

'I have to,' she said, desperation echoing in her voice. 'I have to, David. I can't allow myself to get close to anyone because it makes me vulnerable, and I can't let that happen. Not again.'

For a long time he stood there looking at her, then he drew her into his arms and hugged her gently. 'I won't hurt you. Either of you. I promise that. We can take this as slowly as you want, be as discreet as you like. You can back off at any time. But, please, give us a chance. We could have something so special here, Julia. Something lasting. Don't close the door on it without knowing what it is you're walking away from.'

He kissed her, just a feathering of his lips across her forehead, and then he turned and strode down the hall, picking up his coat on the way, and she heard the soft click of the front door behind him.

It was the loneliest sound in the world.

CHAPTER SIX

JULIA went onto the ward in the morning in a dither of nervous anticipation. She wanted to see David but, although she'd spent the whole night thinking about it, she still wasn't sure she dared to test their relationship.

There just seemed to be too much at stake, although the urge to trust him was sometimes overwhelming. If she could only hand over her responsibilities, just for a while, or share them, even—just to take the pressure off. It was so, so tempting—but then she'd remember Andrew, and how she'd trusted him, and how he'd changed after Katie's birth, and then she'd realise the stakes were too high.

It was just hormones leading her astray again, she thought, like they had with Andrew. He'd been charming to her at first, flirtatious and teasing, then putting the pressure on more and more, but so skilfully that she'd tumbled into bed with him without a second thought.

He'd taught her more about her body than she could have imagined, but his heart had never seemed to be involved, and after a while she'd found it mechanical and unsatisfying. Then she'd had Katie, and his demands had seemed to increase and become even less sensitive to her needs.

And now David was pushing the same buttons, and awakening feelings she'd all but forgotten, and she was afraid to get back on the merry-go-round in case the same thing happened.

It didn't stop her heart from reacting every time she heard his voice, though, or her skin from shivering every time he was near. Common sense seemed to have deserted her where he was concerned, and she had to struggle to keep her mind on the job that morning.

What would he say when he saw her? Would he bring the subject up again, or leave it for her to make the next move?

And if so, what move would she make?

She went to see Mr Burrows, who'd been fretting in the night according to the report, and he was anxious to see David.

'I'd like to talk to him,' he said. 'Will he be round today?'

'I'm sure he will,' she told him. 'I know he intended to talk to you as soon as you were feeling a little brighter. I'll contact him if he doesn't come down in the next hour, all right?'

Mr Burrows nodded. 'I just want the uncertainty to end,' he said frankly. 'I just need to know, one way or the other.'

'I'll make sure he comes,' Julia assured him. She made him comfortable, tried not to think about David and went back to the work station to see who was on the list for Nick Sarazin that day.

'Morning, gorgeous.'

She jumped, caught unawares by David's quiet footsteps, drowned out by the hubbub of the ward. 'Morning,' she said, turning round with a smile coming naturally to her lips. 'And it's Sister Revell to you.'

'Sorry, Sister.' He smiled, but he looked preoccupied, she thought, cocking her head on one side.

'What's the matter?' she asked softly.

He sighed, his smile fleeting and a little sad. 'Mr Burrows. He's been fretting in the night, apparently. My SHO didn't know what to tell him. I need to talk to him now and let him know the score—could you come, too?'

'Sure. He was asking for you a minute ago. I was going to page you, actually, but I was fairly sure you'd be here soon.'

'Is he over the anaesthetic?'

She shrugged. 'Ish. It was quite a long op, wasn't it? He's still feeling a little groggy, but that could be the pain relief. Whatever, he wants to know what you found.'

David dragged a hand through his hair and sighed again. 'I hate doing this. It doesn't matter how many times I have to do it, it never gets any easier. In fact, I think it gets harder, because you're more than ever aware of just what you're telling them.'

'I think he knows.'

He nodded. 'So do I—but thinking you know and being told are two different things. Until I talk to him, he'll still have a lingering glimmer of hope. My words will extinguish it, and he'll have to start the grieving process.

Still, it has to be done. Let's see how gently I can do it.'

Very, Julia was to discover. He was kind and patient and answered all Mr Burrows's questions about the surgery and what he'd found. And then he asked the final question.

'I'm going to die, aren't I?' he said, and David nodded slowly.

'Yes. I'm afraid, ultimately, you are. The oncologist will talk to you about the palliative care he can give you—that's treatment to hold the cancer at bay for as long as possible and keep you comfortable, but at the end of the day that's all we can do now. I'm very, very sorry.'

Mr Burrows nodded pensively. 'I thought as much. Well, thank you for being honest. I need to know—things to do at home, you know? Preparing. Don't want to leave a muddle for the family to sort out. Still, at least the pension's taken care of and my wife won't have to worry about money or the house, and my children are all taken care of— I don't have to feel guilty for letting them down, at least.'

He cracked then, his face crumpling and his shoulders heaving, and Julia perched on the edge of the bed and put her arms round him and held him while he cried. He didn't indulge himself for long, just a few moments to release his pent-up emotions, and then he pulled himself together and apologised. He scrubbed away the tears on his cheeks with the back of his hand, and Julia gave him a tissue and they left him alone for a while to come to terms with his news.

Julia found herself tearing up a little as they left the room, and David shot her an understanding look, propelled her gently into her office and hugged her. 'OK?' he murmured after a moment, and she nodded into his shoulder.

'Yes. It just seems so hard—he's such a nice man, all he's worried about is that his family don't have to suffer or worry.'

Unlike Andrew, who had never given that a moment's thought. Odd, how men could be so different.

'Death, or impending death, tends to bring out the real person, I've found,' David said quietly. 'It's amazing how the silliest people

seem to have huge inner strength, and the ones
you'd expect to cope go completely to pieces.'

'I wonder how his wife will be.'

'I don't know. I'll come back and talk to
him again later. He's bound to have more
questions. Perhaps you'll keep an eye on him
and talk to him if he needs reassurance.'

'Of course. Do you want to see his wife?'

He shrugged. 'We'll play it by ear. He may
have definite views on what he wants her told.
We have to respect that.' He eased away from
her and looked down into her face, his eyes
searching hers. 'You OK now?'

She nodded, smiling self-consciously. 'I'm
just a softie.'

'I noticed. That's fine by me. There aren't
nearly enough softies in the world. Everyone's
busy being hard and tough and independent.
We need to lean on each other.'

'That's fine until you lean on someone and
they aren't there any more,' Julia pointed out.

'I'm here—and I'm going nowhere,' he said
softly. 'Actually, that's a lie. I'm going to my
clinic. I'll see you later. Ring me if you need
me.'

She nearly laughed out loud at that, but stopped herself in time and produced what she hoped was a sensible smile. 'Will do.'

She watched him go, his long stride eating up the corridor as he headed towards Outpatients, and she turned back to her work with her heart in turmoil again.

'I'm here—and I'm going nowhere,' he'd said. Could she dare to believe him?

'Mummy, it's time to go! I'm going to be late!'

'No, you aren't. David said he'd drive us there and then park his car somewhere and come back. He'll be here,' Julia promised, trying to inject confidence into her voice, but it was hard. Andrew had always been late, arriving with a cheerful excuse and brushing aside her concerns.

She checked her watch. David was late— only three minutes, but they were cutting it fine as it was. If they left now, they could just about walk there in time. Any later—

The peal of the doorbell cut across her fretting, and she whisked the door open to find

David there, looking apologetic. 'Sorry I'm on the drag—I had to go back and talk to Mr and Mrs Burrows. Are you both ready?'

She nodded, hating herself for having doubted him. 'Yes. Are you all right for tonight, or do you need to go back to the hospital?'

'No, not tonight. I'm OK.' He smiled past her at Katie. 'All ready, littlest lamb?'

She nodded and giggled. 'Yup.'

'Let's go, then.'

He bundled them into his car, settled Katie on the new booster seat that seemed to have appeared as if by magic in the back of it, and slid behind the wheel. Three minutes later they were at the school, and Julia pointed out the entrance he should come through when he came back.

'I'll go and get her ready and come back to meet you,' she promised, and they left him on the kerb and ran inside. There was a fine drizzle falling, and they arrived in the hall slightly damp and breathless, just as the year-one teacher was calling for her lambs and shepherds.

'Anything I can do?' Julia asked, but she was cheerfully dismissed and sent off to enjoy herself, so she kissed Katie for good luck and went back out to wait for David, arriving at the door just as he did.

'That was quick!' she exclaimed, and he chuckled.

'I had a stroke of luck. There was a space just around the corner, so I nabbed it. Thought it would be easier for afterwards.'

'Absolutely. Come on in, we need to find a seat.'

They were just settling themselves down, and she was wondering if she'd get away without having to see anyone she knew, when Nick and Ronnie Sarazin appeared and waved. Nick did a mild double-take at David, and they squeezed into the row behind them.

'Hello, David,' Nick said, eyeing him assessingly. 'I didn't know you had children here.'

'I don't. I'm here with Julia,' he said, deadpan, and Julia's heart sank. Of all the people to meet, it had to be them! Now there was no chance of keeping it quiet in the hospital.

Nick eyed her thoughtfully, then smiled. 'Good. About time. Ronnie, I don't believe you've met David Armstrong. David, my wife Veronica.'

'Ronnie, please,' she said with a grin, and shook his hand. 'Nice to meet you.'

'So, how did Julia talk you into coming to this dreadful thing?' Nick asked, *sotto voce,* and David chuckled while Ronnie told him off.

'It's not dreadful! It'll be lovely.'

'You're just a softie. They'll all forget their lines.'

'And you'll get pink-eye like you always do.'

Nick coloured slightly and gave a rueful grin. 'Very likely. So?' he added, looking pointedly at David.

'So I'm a sucker,' David said with a smile. 'Katie asked me. I couldn't refuse a beautiful girl, could I, now?'

'Evidently not,' Nick murmured, and his eyes met Julia's and twinkled.

'We're just friends,' she said firmly, and Nick snorted softly and sat back in his seat.

'If you say so.'

They were spared any further discussion by the dimming of the lights and the arrival on stage of one of the older pupils reading the usual passage from the Bible about the decree from Caesar Augustus that all the world should be taxed.

Then the curtains opened and there were children milling around on the stage, making preparations for the journey.

It was a colourful little pageant, with all the usual mishaps. A headdress skidded sideways and fell off, one of the shepherds wet himself, a lamb cried and had to leave the stage, and the innkeeper forgot his only line, but apart from that it was perfect, and at the end David clapped as loudly as any of the fathers.

There were refreshments in the back of the hall while they waited for the children to change and come out. They stood with Nick and Ronnie, and Julia tried to avoid the interested looks of the other mothers.

Not that she'd escape for long, she knew that. The next time they were waiting to pick up the children at the end of the day, Julia knew the questions would start. In fact, she was surprised they were holding back now, some of them!

Then Katie came skipping out and threw herself at David, and with the reflexes of a tried and tested uncle he scooped her up into his arms and plonked a kiss on her cheek. 'Well done, lambkin,' he said, and hugged her.

'Did you see me?' she asked, holding herself away from him so she could see his face.

'Yes, I saw you. You were near the front.'

'Next to Daniel—he cried.' She said it with all the disgust of a five-year-old, and Julia saw David's lips twitch.

The two Sarazin children came running up then, a boy and a girl with Nick's laughing eyes, and he put an arm around each and hugged them. 'Well done, kids,' he said, and then the party broke up and they headed for the door.

The drizzle had turned to mist, and their breath fogged on the cold air. The streetlights made orange haloes high above them, and Julia was glad David was there with them. It was a little creepy, like something out of a Sherlock

Holmes film, and she found herself moving closer to him, Katie between them.

'Here's the car,' he said, flicking the remote control and lighting up the interior with a welcoming glow. Moments later they were on their way home, and as they pulled up outside Julia looked across at him, her heart in her mouth.

'Coffee?' she said, and he smiled slightly.

'I'm starving, I haven't eaten yet. I was going to go and get something. Have you had supper?'

She nodded. 'I had scrambled eggs with Katie at five.'

'Could you force anything else down?'

She smiled. 'Possibly. What did you have in mind?'

'A Chinese take-away?'

Her mouth watered. 'I can always find room for a Chinese,' she confessed, and he grinned.

'I'll see you in a few minutes, then. Any preferences?'

She shook her head. 'None—just lots of fried rice. I love it.'

'OK.'

She took Katie in and put her straight to bed, still excited but almost asleep on her feet. 'Was I all right?' she asked her mother as she snuggled under the quilt.

'You were lovely,' Julia said honestly. 'I was very proud of you. You were the best lamb.' That last was probably poetic licence and maternal pride, but Julia didn't care. She kissed the baby-soft cheek and went downstairs, lit the fire in the sitting room and put the kettle on.

If she'd had a bottle of wine she would have opened it, but she didn't, and anyway David was driving. She found a bottle of mineral water in the cupboard and put it in the fridge in the ice compartment, and then found herself looking in the mirror and finger-combing her hair.

Her heart was pattering in her throat, and when the doorbell rang a moment later she felt it stop for a second.

She closed her eyes for a moment and drew a steadying breath, then walked down the hall and opened the door.

'Here we are,' he said, holding a carrier bag up for her inspection. 'Special fried rice, sweet and sour king prawns, beef in ginger and spring onions, pancake rolls and prawn crackers. Oh, and banana fritters for pudding.'

She laughed in astonishment. 'Good grief, we'll be huge!'

'Speak for yourself. I'm ravenous. Where's the little one?'

'In bed. She was bushed.'

He followed her down to the kitchen, and they put the dishes out on a tray and took them through to the breakfast room with the still tepid mineral water. She'd laid the table with cutlery, but he produced chopsticks from the bag and insisted they use them.

'Everything will be frozen by the time I can eat it!' she wailed, but he just laughed and showed her how to hold them, and then came round behind her and held her fingers in the right position and fed her a prawn. She felt the heat of his body against her shoulders and a deep ache started inside her.

'I think I can manage,' she said breathlessly, and for a second he didn't move. Then he dropped his hand to her shoulder and squeezed it gently before going round to the other side.

He sat opposite her, watching her and laughingly teasing her when she dropped things, and she had more fun eating that meal than she'd had in years. She laughed so much she could hardly pick anything up, and in the end David took pity on her and fed her, and the atmosphere changed, becoming charged with the most incredible tension.

He fed her the banana fritter from a spoon, and when the syrup dribbled down her chin he wiped it up with a fingertip and then put it in her mouth. Her eyes closed on a moan, and she curled her tongue around his fingertip and suckled it gently.

He gave a low groan, and she opened her eyes and met his in a blaze of heat, and her breath jammed in her throat.

She lifted her hand and took his in it, their fingers meshing, and she looked at him and said unsteadily, 'What's happening to us, David?'

'Nothing you don't want,' he murmured, but that didn't help her, because she wanted him, even though she was afraid it might turn into another dreadful mistake.

'I don't know what I want,' she said honestly.

'I know.' His hand turned and cupped her cheek, and he brushed his thumb gently over her cheek in a soothing, rhythmical gesture that slowed her heart and steadied her trembling limbs. 'OK now?' he murmured, and she nodded.

'How about a cup of coffee before I go?' he said, and she nodded again wordlessly and went through into the kitchen and put the kettle on.

'I lit the fire,' she told him in a strained voice. 'I thought we could go into the sitting room.'

'OK.'

He helped her clear up while the kettle boiled, and then they took their mugs through to the sitting room and she looked at the sofa and the chairs and hesitated.

'Sit here with me,' he said, taking the initiative and settling himself into one end of the sofa.

Julia sat at the other end, tucking her feet under her bottom and hunching over her mug, and he put out a hand and caressed her toes where they peeped out from under her thigh. Gradually she relaxed and wriggled down a little, so that his hand rested across her foot and the backs of his fingers touched her thigh, the heat of them scorching her.

'Thank you for letting me come to the nativity play,' he said softly after a while. 'It was fun.'

'You must be a masochist,' she said with a little laugh. 'But thanks for coming. Katie was delighted to have you there. I think she misses having a father figure to parade on these occasions.'

She wondered as she said it if he'd think she was hinting, but it was highly unlikely in view of her reluctance to get involved with him. In fact, it was the first time she'd thought of it herself, and she wondered suddenly how much of Katie's invitation had, in fact, stemmed from that. Surely not.

'Don't worry about it,' he said, reading her mind. 'It was just a nativity play. I'm sure lots of children's parents brought guests.'

But male guests—eligible, single, personable male guests? 'I don't want her building up her hopes,' she said worriedly. 'If she gets some ridiculous idea into her head that we're about to get married and starts telling her friends you're her new daddy—'

'Would it be so ridiculous?' he said softly, and her jaw dropped.

'Don't be daft—I hardly know you!'

David shrugged, and for an instant she thought she saw a vulnerability in his eyes that frightened her. Oh, no. Was he taking this more seriously than she'd realised?

'Whatever,' he said evenly. 'I shouldn't worry about Katie. You're borrowing trouble. Tell her we're just friends, if she says anything.'

She nodded and turned her attention back to her coffee, but it was cold. She put the mug down, and as she straightened up again he reached out and caught her hand.

'Come here,' he coaxed, and she was helpless against the gruff appeal of his voice.

She went into his arms, and he kissed her slowly, lingeringly, moving her so that she lay across his lap, her head cradled on his arm and his head bent over her. His lips were gentle but thorough, and she felt heat building in her.

I shouldn't be doing this, she thought, but she couldn't help herself. Her fingers threaded through his hair, drawing him down against her, and he shifted so that his chest lay against hers and she could feel the ragged rise and fall of his ribs and the thunder of his heart on hers.

'You taste amazing,' he murmured, plundering her mouth again, and she almost wept with need.

Touch me, she wanted to cry, and as if he'd heard her, his hand came up and cupped her breast, the fingers firm but gentle. 'Oh, lord, Julia, stop me,' he whispered, but she couldn't. His hand slid under her blouse, finding the edge of her bra and working its way underneath, so that his hot, hard palm cupped the tender mound.

His breath scorched her face, his eyes burning into hers, and with a ragged groan he took her mouth again in a kiss that threatened to rage out of control.

I want him, she thought with the last coherent remnant of her mind. I want him...

Julia forgot about Katie upstairs, forgot about Andrew, forgot about caution and all the reasons why it was such a bad idea. All she could think of was David and getting closer to him.

And then he lifted his head and eased his hand away, and cradled her against his heaving chest, and as the heat cooled slightly, so common sense returned and she realised what she was doing.

Mortified, she struggled out of his arms and stood up, hugging her arms around her waist. She would have given him anything—anything! What had happened to her?

'Julia, don't,' he said softly. He had moved to stand behind her, and his hands cupped her shoulders and drew her back against him. 'It's all right.'

'I'm behaving like a desperate widow,' she said in a high, cracked voice. 'That is *so* awful.'

'No, you're not. You're behaving like a woman. A real, live, hot-blooded woman. You've done nothing wrong, nothing to be ashamed of.'

'Only because you stopped,' she said, horrified at herself. 'I was—'

'What? Aroused? That's not a sin.'

She turned and forced herself to meet his eyes. 'Oh, yes, it is. I've got a daughter upstairs. I forgot that.'

'I didn't.'

'We could have—oh, lord.'

'No, we couldn't. I wouldn't have done that. Not with Katie in the house.'

Julia moved out of his arms and went to the window, parting the curtains and staring out into the night. 'I think you should go,' she said in a strangled voice. 'Please. I didn't mean this to happen.'

'Julia, stop torturing yourself,' he said softly. 'I'll go, but not because anything will happen if I stay. It won't. I promise you. Not until you decide in the cold light of day that you want it to.'

David drew her into his arms and kissed her tenderly, then he went out into the hall. She heard him putting on his coat and collecting his keys, then the soft click of the front door, and she watched through the gap in the curtains as he went down her path and away from her.

She could still feel the heated throb of her body, the gnawing ache of frustration. There was only one thing that would take it away, and it was the one thing she couldn't allow herself to have. She'd decided long ago that love was a luxury she couldn't afford, and nothing had happened to change that.

It was just that now, it seemed a harder sacrifice to make...

So near, and yet so far.

David drove around the block and pulled up a short distance down the road, and watched as the sitting-room light went out and Julia's bedroom light came on a few moments later.

He tried not to think about what she was doing, or what she'd look like without her clothes, but it was next to impossible.

'You're turning into a peeping Tom,' he growled at himself, but he couldn't drive away until that light was off and he knew she was settled for the night.

It was about five minutes before she switched it off, leaving the house almost in darkness. He could just see the slight glow of a light through the front door, probably the landing light reflecting down the stairs, and after a minute or two he started the car and drove slowly home to the cottage.

He made himself a cup of tea, but he didn't want it. What he wanted was Julia, and he couldn't have her.

Not yet, and maybe not ever.

He was frustrated, unhappy and totally at a loss to know how to proceed. He was falling for her, hard. He'd hoped when he'd met her that she was the right woman for him, and he knew now that she was, just as he knew the sun would rise in the east. He also knew that she was still running scared, and if he could have got his hands on that husband of hers, he would have killed him.

Fortunately the bastard had saved him the effort, probably the only decent thing he'd done in his whole life.

'Oh, Julia,' he said softly in despair, and dropped his head back against the sofa. He could smell her perfume on his sweater, just a light touch of fragrance that seemed uniquely her, and it tormented his already tortured body.

If only he could convince her that he was different, but he couldn't. It would just take time, and he was going to have to tough it out.

There was no way he was going to sleep, he realised. It wasn't even worth trying, so he changed into his work clothes, got out the grouting compound and the squeegee and went into the bathroom. A bit of hard work might settle his libido, if nothing else—and once it was done he could start using the shower.

Cold.

Oh, rats.

CHAPTER SEVEN

'MUMMY, can we see the puppies again soon?'

Julia's heart sank. It was all she needed after her restless night, but Katie had talked about almost nothing else since the weekend, and she knew just how much the little girl would have loved a dog of her own.

If their circumstances had been different, Julia would have loved one as well, but as it was, it just wouldn't be fair, and anyway, Arthur would no doubt object violently.

'Maybe we can go and see them in a day or two,' she stalled, but Katie understood that for what it was and her optimistic little face fell.

'I knew you wouldn't let me go back,' she said, 'and I've got to go to Granny and Grandpa Revell this weekend, so I can't see them then, and after that it's Christmas and the puppies are going—'

'What about my morning off?' Julia suggested, weakening. 'You break up tomorrow, and on Friday I don't have to be at work until twelve, so we could go before you go to Granny and Grandpa, if you like—if Mrs Armstrong doesn't mind.' And David will be at work, she thought, so it'll be safe.

'Ring her,' Katie pleaded, but Julia shook her head. 'Darling, it's only twenty to seven in the morning, and we have to go now, anyway, or I'll be late for work. I'll ring her tonight.'

'Promise,' Katie said, and her mother promised.

She dropped her at the childminder who looked after her before school, and then pulled up in the car park at the hospital just as David was getting out of his car.

'Hi,' he said soberly, and she looked at him, at the shadows round his eyes and the tiredness on his face, and thought he'd possibly had an even worse night than her.

'Hi,' she said, and tried for a smile.

He didn't smile back. Instead he came over to her and stood in silence for a moment, then rammed a hand through his hair. 'Look, about last night—things got out of hand. I didn't mean to push you. I know you wanted to take things slowly, and I rushed you. I'm sorry.'

Her silly heart ached for him. 'Don't be sorry. You didn't do anything I didn't want you to do. That's the problem. I just think— oh, I don't know. It would be so easy to go too far, too fast, and I don't want Katie hurt.'

'I know. I realise that.'

'She wants to see the puppies again,' she told him. 'I don't suppose your mother would let us go over on Friday morning, would she? I don't have to be in until late, and Katie's on holiday from tomorrow.'

He grinned a little lopsidedly. 'I'm sure she'd love it. I was wondering, actually, if you want to go over there this afternoon, after I finish. I thought maybe Mum could babysit and we could go out for a drink and talk.'

'Is there anything to talk about?' she asked, trying not to let herself get excited at the thought.

David's smile was wry. 'I don't know. I hope so. I thought we should go somewhere safe and chaperoned, and just talk a bit. We only seem to see each other at work, or in front of Katie, or when we're alone and then we get distracted. That's making it difficult for us to do the normal getting-to-know-each-other things, and I'd like to find out more about you—find out what makes you tick.'

'There's not much to know,' she said, thinking of what a narrow life she led, but he shook his head reprovingly.

'Nonsense. Will you? Would Katie like that?'

'Katie would be ecstatic,' she said drily.

'And you?'

I'd be ecstatic, too, Julia thought, but she wasn't telling him that! 'I dare say I could tolerate it,' she said with a smile, and he winked at her.

'Good girl,' he said approvingly.

She stood there for a second, just enjoying the smile in his eyes, and then collected herself with a start.

'What am I thinking about? I'll be late—I can't stand here chatting!'

'Any chance of a cup of tea?'

'What—now you've made me late?' She laughed, running towards the door. 'What do you think?'

He followed her, going into the kitchen and putting the kettle on while she took report from Angie Featherstone, and then he came into the office and handed her a mug of tea, settling himself down on the other side of the desk with his own mug and a lazy smile.

'So, anything exciting happen in the night?' he asked.

'Not really. You've got something white on your eyebrow, by the way. It looks like paint.'

He stood up and went over to the little mirror behind the door, and picked at the white mark.

'Grout,' he said in disgust, and she stifled a laugh.

'Grout?' she echoed, and he gave her a black look in the mirror.

'You heard.'

She couldn't hold back the smile, but neither could he, and they ended up laughing together. It felt good, she thought in surprise. Natural.

Wonderful, actually.

'What time tonight?' she asked, suddenly looking forward to their drink.

'I should be able to get away about six. We shouldn't be too late really, because of Katie, I suppose. Mum could feed her, and we could have a meal in the pub. Does that sound OK?'

'It sounds good.'

'I'll pick you up after I finish, then. I must go. I've got some paperwork to do with my secretary this morning and I want to look through the notes again. Do I need to see anyone on the ward while I'm here?'

Julia shook her head. 'Not that I know of. Your registrar or SHO should be able to cope today. I'll see if Mr Burrows is all right—he's the only one I'm worried about. Do you think he should be talking to the oncologist now?'

He nodded. 'Probably. He'll take over treatment as soon as Mr Burrows has healed from the surgery. I'll ring him and have a word— perhaps we'll talk to him together. Whatever. I'll see you later. Ring me if you want me.'

That again, she thought, but this time she smiled. They were going out together somewhere safe, where they could just talk, and perhaps that was just what they needed. A chance to get to know each other without being distracted by their hormones. And maybe, just maybe, she might learn to trust him.

The phone rang, distracting her from her thoughts. It was A and E, to say that an elderly lady suffering from a perforated bowel had been admitted directly to Theatre, and to stand by to expect her.

She put the phone down and was on her way to shuffle beds to make room when Nick Sarazin came onto the ward.

'Ah, Julia,' he said, and her heart sank. He was the last person she needed to see after bumping into him last night at the nativity play. Judging by the sparkle in his eyes, he wasn't about to allow her to get away with it.

'I gather you've got an admission from A and E,' she said, trying to head him off, but he wouldn't be deflected.

'Yes, I'm going up now. I was just coming to warn you but someone's done it. I'll fit her in first, obviously.' He cocked his head on one side and smiled at her inquisitively. 'So, you and David—what's the story?'

'No story. He's a friend,' she said firmly, but one brow shot up into a disbelieving arch and he snorted under his breath.

'Pull the other. He couldn't take his eyes off you.'

'Really?' she said lightly. 'I didn't notice.'

'Then you must be more dead than alive,' he retorted, but he seemed to relent, his tone gentling. 'He's a nice guy, Julia. You might do worse than to give him a chance.'

'We know very little about him,' she pointed out.

'That's rubbish. He went to a nativity play, for heaven's sake, because your daughter asked him to. He comes in early to talk to patients, and stays late if necessary. He likes children and animals. He's kind. What more could you want to know?'

'How do you know he likes animals?' she said sharply, and Nick laughed.

'I don't. I'm just guessing. Am I right?'

She coloured and laughed despite herself. 'Yes, dammit, you are.'

'So there. I rest my case—and now I'm off to Theatre. See you later.'

He left the ward and she went on her bed hunt, running her conversation with Nick through her mind. Had David really been unable to take his eyes off her? She'd thought he'd been watching the play, but she'd been so busy watching it herself she couldn't be sure. And Nick was right—David was a kind person.

Which was more than could ever have been said about Andrew!

Still, it was a big step to take, and she'd need more than kindness to convince her to take it.

Her bed-shuffling done, she went to see Mr Burrows and found him propped up on his pillows, writing something on a spiral-bound notepad. She perched on the edge of the bed and smiled at him.

'Hi, there. How are you doing?' she asked, and he smiled back tiredly and shrugged.

'Oh, so-so. Just making lists of things to do. I don't want to forget something important.'

'I think you are forgetting something important,' she said gently. 'You're forgetting to rest.'

'I can't rest—not until I'm sure I've done everything. I have to talk to my solicitor.'

'The oncologist is going to be coming to see you soon about your treatment,' she told him. 'You need to rest and get well enough for that, and it will give you more time to do things afterwards. There's no desperate rush.'

He smiled fretfully at her. 'I know, but I just feel useless lying here, and it takes my mind off it.'

'Can I get you something to do? Maybe the occupational therapist has got something simple you could be doing in a day or two to keep your mind busy. Shall I ask her to come and see you?'

'OK.'

'And you are remembering to do your leg exercises every hour to keep your blood moving in your legs, aren't you?'

'Yes. Well, mostly.'

'Try and remember. Let me check your stockings are up properly,' she said, and straightened the top of one that was threatening to roll down. All the patients wore graduated pressure stockings to prevent the blood pooling and clotting in their legs during and after surgery, and keeping them smooth was one of the banes of her life.

'That's better,' she said, and listened to his abdomen with a stethoscope. 'No bowel sounds yet, are there? Are you feeling any movement? Any wind?'

'I can feel wind inside, but it's not shifting.'

'You'll feel better when it does,' she assured him. 'Your wound's healing nicely, anyway.'

'I suppose I should be grateful for small mercies,' he said with a fleeting smile, and she wondered what it was like to be handed a death sentence at fifty-eight.

Grim.

'I'll get the OT lady to see you when she's next on the ward—and in the meantime you rest, please.'

He put the pad down and sighed. 'I am tired, actually.'

'And in pain. Don't overdo it, it's only your second day post-op and it was major surgery. I'll get one of the health care assistants to come and give you a mouthwash, then I want you to settle down for a sleep, otherwise I'll get Mr Armstrong to write you up for a sedative and we'll make sure you rest.'

He smiled wearily, and she left him with his eyes shut and found someone to go and make him comfortable, because Nick's lady from A and E had come back from Theatre and was needing her attention.

She put Mrs Harrison into the other single room opposite the nursing station, next to Mr Burrows. That way she could keep an eye on her from the nursing station once she didn't need such intensive attention, but in the meantime she'd need specialist nursing from someone designated to the task.

In view of her general frailty, Julia decided to do it herself, and handed the running of the ward over to Sally, her staff nurse.

There were lots of machines to monitor. The intravenous analgesic pump that delivered painkillers at a steady rate, the heart and oxygen monitors, the automatic blood pressure monitor—all had to be watched and checked to make sure they were working properly, and the results noted at regular intervals. Mrs Harrison's temperature was high and needed a constant eye kept on it to make sure it didn't rise.

Then the wound drain, the urinary catheter and IV line all had to be watched for potential problems, and the patient had to be turned and repositioned at regular intervals even though she was on a low air loss bed to prevent pressure sores.

She'd had a temporary colostomy to allow her bowel to recover, and the stoma had to be cared for very carefully until it had healed. There was a stoma nurse who would come and deal with it after the immediate post-op period, but for now it was Julia's job.

Nick came down at lunchtime after his list was finished to check on his patient, and he gave Julia a run-down on her operation.

'She's had diverticular disease for years, apparently, and she'd been feeling rough for a while but hadn't said anything. A neighbour raised the alarm this morning and they found her collapsed in bed. She's lucky to be alive, but she's got raging peritonitis. We may lose her yet. I hope not. I flushed her out with antibiotic solution, and she's got antibiotics IV, but she's pretty weak.'

'She seems to be holding at the moment,' Julia said thoughtfully. 'Some of these elderly ladies are as tough as old boots. They seem indestructible.'

'I know. Well, we can only hope she's one of them. Her daughter's on her way from the Midlands—she should be here any time. I'll come and talk to her if you give me a call when she arrives.'

'OK. Thanks.'

Nick looked out of the door and grinned, then popped his head back inside. 'Lover-boy's here,' he whispered teasingly, and ducked out of the way before she could summon a reply.

She heard him talking to David outside, and her heart fluttered betrayingly. Seconds later David came into the room and smiled, and her heart flipped right over.

Anatomically impossible, but that was what it felt like.

'Hi,' he said softly, and she found herself grinning inanely.

'Hi, yourself. How was your paperwork?'

'Boring. I've left my secretary to deal with it. How are you?'

'Oh, pretty busy. I'm specialling Mrs Harrison here. She had a perforated bowel.'

He nodded. 'I heard. I rang my mother—she's happy for us to drop Katie over there this evening.'

'Oh—right. Thanks.'

'Don't thank me,' he said with a lazy, sexy smile. 'I have a vested interest in this evening.'

'So you do,' she said, her heart skittering again, and she wondered if he'd ever be able to smile at her without doing things to her insides.

'I'll see you later—I'm just going down to my clinic. If it's nice and straightforward, I might even get away early, but don't hold your breath.'

'I won't,' she promised, but in the end she did, of course, haunting the front window from five thirty onwards.

A watched kettle and all that, she thought at five past six, and went into the kitchen to feed the importuning cat again and make sure he had fresh water. 'You're getting fat, Arthur,' she told him, and he mewed tragically at her until she put his dish down. He dived headlong into it and crunched up the food with great enthusiasm. 'Perhaps you've got worms,' she said drily. 'Or maybe you're just a pig.'

Nevertheless, she got David to hold him when he arrived a few minutes later so she could stuff a worming tablet down his throat, just to be on the safe side. She was always very fussy because of Katie, even though she knew she was probably worrying unnecessarily. She wormed Arthur regularly every month after all, which according to the vet should be enough for even the most voracious hunter.

'He's just a big cat,' David reassured her. 'We've got one on the farm that looks like him.'

'Leo,' Katie said authoritatively. 'I've met him. He's even bigger.'

'I think he might be. Right, are we ready?'

Katie hopped excitedly from foot to foot. 'I am, I am. Can we go?'

Julia laughed and ruffled her hair. 'All right, pumpkin. Come on.'

She reached for her coat and found it taken out of her hands and held for her, David's hands snuggling it round her neck before releasing it. Just another of the thoughtful little things he did instinctively, she thought, and stored it away in her mental filing cabinet.

By the time she'd buttoned it he'd got Katie wrapped up in her coat, and he ushered them out to his car and whisked them through the traffic and out into the country on the back roads.

They called in at the cottage so he could change into something less formal and, true to his word, he left them in the car for only two minutes, reappearing in casual cotton trousers and a rugby shirt with a thick sweater over the top.

'That's better. I hate ties,' he said with a grin, and they set off again for the farm.

'Oh, they've grown!' Katie exclaimed as they entered the kitchen and saw the puppies.

'They do. They grow really fast at this age,' Mrs Armstrong said. 'You're just in time to help me feed them, and then you can have supper with us.'

David's father came out of his study to say hello, and Julia couldn't help but notice the natural and friendly way he greeted both her and Katie.

'So, young 'un, how was the nativity play? I gather you were a very wonderful lamb,' he said, and Katie giggled.

'Did David tell you?' she asked, and he nodded.

'Certainly did. I hope we get to see a photo.'

'Oh, they take lots of photos,' Julia assured him. 'No doubt I'll have to buy them all.'

'Of course,' Mrs Armstrong said with a laugh. 'We've got hundreds of such photos—some of them of David. Remind me to show you the baby photos one day.'

'I think not,' David said, colouring slightly, and he ushered Julia towards the door. 'If you two are quite happy for us to go, I think we'll make a move. I feel a steak calling me.'

'Bye, darling,' Julia said, but Katie was in the playpen with the puppies already and hardly spared her a glance.

'So, where are we going?' she asked to break the silence in the car.

'The village pub. It's excellent, and they have a log fire. At this time of night we'll probably be able to get a seat near it in the corner—unless you want to eat in the restaurant?'

'Not really,' she said. 'Well, I don't mind, but I'm not really dressed for formal dining.'

'Nor am I, not now,' he said with what sounded like relief. 'We'll eat in the bar.'

He was right, it was a lovely pub, and the food was wonderful. They tucked themselves away in the corner by the fire, and they talked. David told her about himself—about his training in London, his various jobs around the country, his yearning to be back in his native Suffolk—and he asked Julia about herself.

'You've hardly told me anything about yourself,' he said with gentle reproach. 'You've told me about Andrew, and Katie, but almost nothing about you.'

She shrugged diffidently. 'I'm not that interesting.'

'You are to me.'

He seemed to mean it, so she told him about her childhood in Hampshire, and her parents' move to Lancashire when she was sixteen, a social disaster for her and very unsettling.

'I had to leave all my friends, and it really was very hard, breaking into a new group in the sixth form. I didn't do as well in my A-levels as I'd been expected to and, instead of doing physiotherapy, I ended up on a nursing course, which actually in the end has probably suited me better.'

'So how did you meet Andrew?' he asked quietly, and she sighed.

'Oh, after I'd qualified and got a job nearer home. He was on a fast track to the top, and he'd been posted to Blackburn to run a new branch of the company he worked for. I met him at a friend's house, at a party, and he was funny and charming and he made me feel special.'

Julia fell silent, remembering how easy it had been for him to seduce the almost innocent girl she'd been, and she sighed.

'I take it that didn't last.'

'Only until I had Katie. He changed. Well, no, maybe he didn't, but I did. I was a mother.

I was tired, and my priorities shifted. He didn't like that.'

'Men often don't. They feel neglected.'

'So I found out.' She stopped, not wanting to go on. There were things she didn't want to talk about—the demands he'd made on her, the way he'd expected her to welcome his advances so soon after the birth, the impatience with which he'd greeted her slow recovery.

Andrew had been insatiable, jealous and ever more critical of her figure and performance, both in bed and out of it, and then he'd left her, her confidence in rags, her self-image devastated.

Julia shook her head, remembering, and David squeezed her knee. She glanced up at him and he smiled gently. 'Tell me about you,' he coaxed. 'What's your favourite colour?'

'Silver,' she said, thinking of his eyes, and he smiled again.

'So you like my car, then.'

'Amongst other things. Moonlight. Water. Your eyes.'

'My eyes?'

'They're silver,' she said, and his mouth quirked fleetingly.

'Really?'

'Really.'

'I always thought they were grey.'

'No,' she corrected. 'Mine are grey. Yours are silver.'

'OK. What's your favourite sort of music?'

'Oh, easy. I like cheesy pop music.'

'Good grief,' he said, looking shocked.

'Don't tell me, you're a classical fan,' she teased, and he nodded.

'Absolutely. I like quiet, pure music, like plainsong and church music. Choristers, piano, the flute—simple sounds. Nothing brash.'

She nodded. 'I could probably tolerate that.'

'Big of you.'

She chuckled. 'So, what about you. What's your favourite colour?'

'Green. Soft, willow green, shivering in the breeze. The brilliant acid green of opening leaves in the spring, and rich long grass, and glossy holly leaves—'

'That's about four different greens.'

'Very likely. It's the one colour that was lacking in London, except in the parks, and I didn't have very much time to go and sit in them when I was training. And I hate hospital green with a passion.'

'Ditto,' she said, laughing, and he leant over and kissed her cheek.

'There, we agree on something,' he said, and their eyes meshed and held.

'So, what about films?' he asked.

'*The Horse Whisperer*—and *Elizabeth.*'

'Not *Armageddon?*'

'No. I hate sad films.'

'*The Horse Whisperer* is sad.'

'Well, yes, but it's sort of right.'

'So is *Armageddon.*'

Julia laughed. 'We'll have to agree to differ again.'

Their conversation moved on, touching on medical things and ending with a deep and fundamental disagreement on embryo research. In the end she fell silent, and David cocked his head on one side and looked at her.

'What's the matter?'

She shrugged. 'Nothing.' But it wasn't nothing. They seemed to be differing on a lot of things, she thought, her earlier cheerfulness dwindling. Oh, dear.

She looked up at him and shook her head, dredging up a smile again. 'It's nothing,' she said again, but he seemed to understand.

'It is nothing. Don't worry about it,' he murmured, reading her mind. 'We're allowed to be different. That's what makes the world go round.'

'Thought that was love.'

'Well, that, too,' he said with a grin. 'But I was trying to steer clear of the subject—like sex and politics. Always dangerous.' He glanced at his watch. 'We ought to be going. It's nearly nine, and Katie's got school tomorrow, hasn't she?'

Guilt swamped her. 'Yes—oh, lord, I had no idea it was so late.'

'She'll live. They won't do anything very much at school tomorrow anyway. You never do at the end of term, and particularly not when you're five.'

'Nearly six,' she reminded him. 'She's six in January.'

'I'd better start saving,' he murmured, helping her into her coat. 'No doubt it will cost a fortune to distract her from the idea of a puppy.'

Julia rolled her eyes. 'Well, I'll let you deal with that one,' she said, 'since it's your fault, but I'd be grateful if you didn't spend a fortune on her, as I can't afford to match it.'

David paused in the act of shrugging on his coat, and frowned slightly. 'I was joking,' he said mildly. 'I don't believe in spoiling children—well, not like that, anyway.'

She let out a little sigh. 'Another thing we agree on, then,' she said lightly. 'Come on, let's go while we're winning.'

But it didn't feel like they were winning, and when he dropped her off at the house with a chaste peck on the cheek in deference to Katie's presence, she was if anything more confused than ever…

CHAPTER EIGHT

FORTUNATELY for Julia, Mrs Harrison was still very poorly the following day and so she was able to tuck herself away with the frail patient and watch her closely.

She was still on quarter-hourly observations, and Julia felt she should really have been in ICU, but it wasn't possible because as usual they were full. Besides, she was quite happy to have the opportunity to do a little intensive nursing for a change instead of admin, which seemed to be the way her job was going these days.

Mrs Harrison's daughter was with her, and they talked through her operation and the expected programme of her recovery in between Julia's checking and noting. She didn't really have a minute to herself, which suited her. She had too much time to think these days, and she just wanted some time out. Being closeted with

Mrs H. and her daughter was a good way of doing it.

And, she thought, it had the added advantage of taking her out of circulation, so she could avoid cosy little chats with David.

Or so she hoped, at least. At lunchtime, Sally stuck her head round the door and told her to go for lunch.

'I'll take over. You can't have all the fun— and Mr Armstrong wants you to join him. Said something about a patient conference.'

Julia muttered something disbelieving under her breath and went out to find David lounging against the wall looking expectant.

'Ready? Get your coat.'

'Where are we going and why?' she asked, but he just smiled.

'Secret. Come on.'

'I thought this was a patient conference?' she said mildly, allowing him to engineer her down to the car park entrance.

'Just a ruse to get you into my clutches,' he said with an unrepentant grin. Feeling highly dubious but intrigued for all that, she let him put her into his car, and they drove out into the countryside just minutes away.

There he parked, on a rise looking over a pretty river valley, and with a flourish like a magician he produced a cardboard box from the back seat and put it on the space between their seats.

'*Voilà!*' he said, and she laughed softly.

'What is that?' she asked.

'Lunch. I hate canteen food, and I wanted to talk to you after last night. You looked worried.'

She felt her smile slip. 'We disagreed on so many things.'

'Not that many—and, anyway, we're allowed to disagree. It makes life more interesting.' He opened the carton and peered in. 'Here—prawn salad sandwiches, chicken legs, cherry tomatoes—what's in this little pot? Pasta salad—and plastic forks. We'll have to share. Think we can manage that?'

'I expect so,' she said, peering into the box and suddenly realising how hungry she was.

David picked up a chicken leg and gestured at the box with it as she hesitated. 'Come on, it's not a spectator sport,' he teased, and she helped herself to a sandwich bursting with fat, juicy prawns and crisp shreds of salad.

'So where did this lot come from?' she mumbled with her mouth full.

'A sandwich firm in town. I got them to deliver it.'

That shocked her a little, even though she knew he earned good money and only had himself to spend it on. 'How extravagant,' she scolded mildly, but he shook his head.

'Not really. We have to eat, and they deliver to the hospital anyway. Besides, you aren't supposed to look a gift horse in the mouth and all that. Now eat.'

Julia did, and it was wonderful. She didn't buy his story that it wasn't extravagant, but she was too hungry to care and it was nice to be alone with him, although she'd been trying to forget about him all morning.

Unsuccessfully, she realised.

'You've been hiding from me,' he said, reading her mind again.

'I know. I just wanted some thinking time.'

'And?'

She smiled ruefully. 'I'm still thinking.'

'Want to think out loud?'

She shook her head. 'You won't want to hear it.'

'Andrew again?'

'We had nothing in common,' she told him heavily. 'We differed in so many respects, and I was never allowed an opinion. If I disagreed with him, I was an idiot.'

'Arrogant bastard.'

'You and I disagreed,' she reminded him. 'Last night, about embryo research. We disagreed really quite fundamentally.'

'That doesn't mean you aren't allowed your opinion,' he pointed out, and put a chicken leg in her hand. 'Eat.'

She ate, wondering if he really meant it or if, given time, he'd start to erode her personality as Andrew had done. It was so insidious, that was the trouble. It had taken ages before she'd realised what had been happening to her.

They shared the pasta salad, David feeding them alternate forkfuls, and he opened the bottle of spring water and poured her some into a plastic cup before sitting back with a sigh and looking out over the gently rolling landscape.

'I love this part of Suffolk,' he said softly. 'I really missed it.'

'I missed Hampshire when we moved—the downs near Winchester, the New Forest. It seemed very wet and cold and forbidding in Lancashire after that.'

'I'm sure.' He tilted his head and looked at her searchingly. 'Do you want to go back to Hampshire?'

She shook her head. 'Only to visit. This is my home now, and Katie's home. We've got roots here, even if they are a little damaged from being transplanted so many times.'

'Is that gardening talk?' he teased laughingly, and she smiled.

'You know, I'd love to learn a bit about gardening,' she said wistfully.

'I'll teach you. You can help me at the cottage, if you like, and we can sort your garden out and make it pretty for you.'

She snorted. 'That won't take long, it's only tiny.'

'It could still be lovely, I'm sure. I'll have a look next time I'm there—if you like.'

Yet another thread that would weave them together, she thought, but she found herself agreeing anyway. It was only the garden, after all.

'We ought to get back,' she said, looking at her watch, and David nodded.

'I know, but there's something I want to do first,' he said. Taking the carton, he put it into the back of the car and then drew her into his arms and kissed her.

It was a gentle kiss, almost without passion, but then he lifted his head and looked down into her eyes, and kissed her again.

This kiss was far from gentle. It was a deep, searching kiss, a yearning kiss, and it started an ache inside her that hadn't really gone away since the last time. And this time, when he lifted his head, it wasn't sunshine that gleamed through his quicksilver eyes but desire, hard and hot and urgent, and it turned her to jelly.

'Hell's teeth,' he muttered, and dragged himself back behind the wheel, closing his eyes and dropping his head back against the headrest. 'I have to go back to work. I have a clinic. I have to talk to patients, and all I'm going to be able to think about is you. I'll disgrace myself.'

'It's your fault,' she pointed out, wondering if her heart would slow down before it gave up the unequal struggle and just stopped permanently. 'You didn't have to do that.'

He rolled his head towards her and gave a strangled laugh. 'Oh, yes, I did,' he said softly and, sitting up, he started the engine, clipped on his seat belt and backed out of the gateway, turning back towards Audley and reality.

And not before time, Julia thought with a little bubble of panic.

She almost ran back to the ward, and as she went into Mrs Harrison's room, Sally looked up and her eyes widened.

'Good lunch?' she asked, and Julia nodded.

'You might like to go and sort your hair out—it's falling down,' Sally pointed out, and Julia looked in the mirror over the basin and groaned inwardly. It was a good job Mrs Harrison's daughter was having a lunch break, she thought, because she looked thoroughly and comprehensively kissed.

She pulled the band out of her hair, scraped it back again and twisted it up into a bun, securing it again with another twist of the scrunchie. Better.

She turned and gave Sally a level look. 'I'll take over again now,' she said, and Sally shut her mouth, handed over the charts and left without a word.

Julia said goodbye to Katie the following morning with reluctance. They'd spent a little while at the farm with the puppies, and she'd had coffee with Mrs Armstrong and had tried hard not to get dragged into conversation about David.

When they were leaving, his mother drew her to one side and said softly, 'Think about Christmas. You don't have to decide beforehand. Just come—even if you wake up on Christmas morning and want to come over, you'd be welcome. Or even on Christmas Eve, if you just want to come for a drink in the evening. We'll all be here.'

'Thank you,' Julia murmured, knowing full well she had no intention of joining them at any time but wishing that she could. She removed Katie yet again from the puppies and took her back to the house to wash and change before she left. The Revells picked her up at eleven-thirty, on time for once, and Julia arrived at work for twelve with the knowledge that the weekend stretched ahead of her emptily. She was working on Sunday, but Saturday was a yawning void and she wondered if anyone wanted to swap shifts.

No. She had to do some Christmas shopping with the few pounds she had available. Should she buy David something? If so, she had no idea what. She didn't have enough money to get anything worthwhile, and she couldn't imagine he'd want anything she could make.

Even a cake would be heartily outdone by his mother's everyday offerings.

Oh, rats.

She found Mr Burrows restless and unsettled, and impatient to get on with the remaining months of his life. 'I don't have time to lie here,' he fretted, and she had to talk to him again about resting to speed his recovery.

'If you don't rest, it will take longer, so you'll just have to be patient,' she reminded him, and took his notepad away again. 'Now, lie back and count sheep or something.'

'I'll count bullying nurses,' he said with a smile, and Julia squeezed his hand and left him to it, going into the room next door to see Nick's patient with the perforated bowel.

Mrs Harrison seemed to have turned the corner with her peritonitis, and Julia was pleased to see her daughter sitting with her again. She was waking up more now and talking, and her daughter sat beside her with her knitting and chatted to her when she was awake. The rhythmic clicking of the needles seemed to comfort the elderly woman when she had her eyes closed, because she knew her daughter was still there by her side.

She didn't need observing so closely now, but she still needed checking every half hour and turning and, of course, she had to have the physio to keep her chest and legs moving.

'Wiggle your feet for me,' Julia would say every half-hour when she turned her, and Mrs Harrison would move her feet a little to help pump the blood back from her calves.

She got the daughter in on the act, and she proved to be a most useful helper, and reliable enough for some of the routine tasks to be handed over to her.

'How long are you here for?' Julia asked.

'Till Christmas. She was coming to us, but I don't suppose she can now. I've got the children coming with their other halves and the grandchildren, so I have to go back home, but I'll be back again afterwards if she needs me, and she can come to us to convalesce.'

'I won't need to come to you, I'll be going home,' Mrs Harrison said confidently, but Julia wasn't so sure. Her recovery was going to be long and slow. She was nearly eighty, after all, and she'd been extremely ill. Still, time would tell.

The end of her shift came with the arrival of Angie Featherstone, and she handed over and went home to a house that seemed empty and bleak. She'd need to buy a tree ready to put up with Katie on Christmas Eve, and she had to go shopping for food for Christmas and also presents.

She'd done the presents from Katie to her grandparents, and presents to her own parents and siblings had been posted ages ago, but she still hadn't got anything for Katie.

Or David.

She tried to watch television, but there was nothing on that caught her attention, so she made a hot drink and went to bed, and early the next morning she got up and walked down into town to do her Christmas shopping. It was Saturday, two and a half shopping days to Christmas, and already by nine o'clock it was heaving.

It was a horrible day, cold and damp with a blustery wind that cut right through her, and she ducked from shop to shop, fruitlessly searching for anything to give either Katie or David. Time after time she drew a blank, and just when she was despairing of ever finding anything, she saw an old print of Little Soham, with David's cottage in it, in the window of an art shop in the middle of town.

It was perfect, and she was just going through the door to ask for it when a sudden gust of wind caught her and pushed her against the wall. People laughed and leant into the wind, hats and scarves flying, and then suddenly there was a grinding, tearing noise and the laughter turned to screams of terror as the tarpaulin-clad scaffolding on the front of a shop toppled slowly outwards and crashed down onto the packed precinct.

There was the sound of splintering plate-glass windows, and flying glass hurtled through the air in all directions, slashing through the panicked crowd and cutting them down like ninepins.

For a moment there was shocked silence, and then the screams started.

'Oh, my God,' Julia whispered, her skin crawling with horror, and as she looked around she saw blood everywhere.

'Call the emergency services!' she snapped. 'Tell them it's a major incident and they'll need medical teams out here fast.'

'Right,' the man behind the counter said, startled, and she ran out into the street. Oh, lord, where to start?

People were running round in panic, crawling on the ground and cutting themselves trying to find their relatives, and the screaming was horrendous.

Then a deep, authoritative voice cut through the panic and silenced them.

'Everybody keep still! Stop moving and wait for help to come to you. If anyone has any first-aid experience, please come over here.'

'David,' she said, relief flooding through her, and she picked her way across to him. 'I'm here,' she said, and he closed his eyes for a moment, then opened them again and gave her a shaky smile.

'Good,' he said, and he sounded stunned for a moment, then pulled himself together. 'Start with triage. There are some hideous injuries— and mind the blood. Remember the risks.'

'I'm a nurse,' someone said, and another woman ran up and said she was a GP. Someone from a pharmacy brought out a box of latex gloves, and the first aid volunteers helped themselves, then looked to David for further instructions.

'Come with me,' Julia said, and they waded into the sobbing crowd, scanning for priority cases.

'Help me,' people were saying, but they could only do so much, and when the sirens sounded just moments later, Julia heaved a sigh of relief.

David and a group of strong men had lifted the scaffolding off the people trapped under it, propping it up on things dragged from shops to support the poles so rescue workers could get underneath and assess the injuries.

Now she could see him working on some-one just a few feet away, and he lifted his head and hailed the paramedics.

'Major arterial bleed here,' he said, and they ran over to him and relieved him so that he could continue with his triage.

He scanned the area and beckoned Julia, who had just tied a scarf tightly round a bleed-ing arm to staunch the flow.

'What is it?' she asked, and he drew her into the shop immediately opposite the scaffolding, where they picked their way carefully over the shattered glass.

The shop had been packed, and as the ends of the poles had come through the window the glass had flown in and caused mayhem.

'This isn't going to be nice,' he warned, and she looked around and her hand came up to cover her mouth.

'Oh, lord,' she said, gagging slightly.

'Come on,' he said bracingly. 'You've seen worse.'

She wasn't sure that she had. Following him and trying to scrape together her professionalism, she stepped over the decapitated body of a woman and followed him into the devastated interior.

They worked for nearly an hour, and then David decided they'd be more use at the hospital. 'They'll need emergency surgical teams,' he told her. 'We could open up a theatre—will you scrub for me? Have you got time?'

'Sure,' she said, all too ready to get back to the clinical order of the hospital instead of the pandemonium of the shattered street.

Within half an hour they were in Theatre, repairing the damage done by flying glass and shattered shopfittings. Some of the injuries were straightforward, others much more complicated and life-threatening.

Pregnant women, terrified children, old men who'd lost their wives in the chaos and were worried to death—all came through their hands and were repaired and sent off to be slotted into corridors and odd nooks and crannies and sorted out by the police and medical social workers so they could be reunited with their loved ones.

They were working until nearly six that night with only a short break between cases while the theatre was cleaned, and by the time the last casualty was stitched up and put to bed they were dropping with exhaustion.

'Come on,' David said firmly to her as she slumped in the changing room. 'I'm taking you home.'

'My clothes are covered in blood,' she told him, almost in a trance.

'Stay in your scrubs. My car'll warm up fast.'

She nodded. 'I need to have a shower, but I just want to get out of here.'

'Me, too. Let's go to your place and pick up some clothes, and then go over to the cottage and wash and change and have something to eat. You don't need to be alone this evening and neither do I.'

She nodded again and went with him, content to let him take over. She felt too tired and shocked to argue, and her house was too empty without Katie. She grabbed a few things from her bedroom and ran back down, fed Arthur and went back out to David's warm car with a feeling of relief.

It was cosy and safe and there was something hugely comforting about his presence.

The cottage when they got there was warm, because the woodburner had been alight earlier and the embers were still glowing.

'You go and shower,' he told her firmly, 'I'll get the fire going and start supper.'

Julia ran upstairs and went into the bath-room and turned on the taps, but the water ran with blood and she stared at it and started to cry helplessly, great shaking sobs that racked her body and ripped through her, tearing her apart.

'Julia? Let me in. Julia!'

She stumbled to the door and opened it, fall-ing into David's arms, and he held her tight and rocked her wordlessly.

'It's the blood,' she wept. 'All I can see is the blood.'

'It's all right,' he soothed, and, leading her back into the bathroom, he perched on the side of the bath and turned off the taps, then pulled her down onto his lap, cradling her against his chest. 'Shh. It's all right. I've got you.'

She shuddered in his arms, and his hands came up and rubbed her shoulders soothingly.

'It was just so awful,' she said emptily. 'Just before Christmas. Those poor people.'

'I thought you were under it,' he said. 'I'd seen you a moment before, and then I lost you in the crowd. When it came down...'

He broke off, his arms tightening, and she slid her arms around his chest and hugged him back. 'I'm fine. I'm here.'

'I know.'

He lifted her to her feet and stood up, then peeled the top of her scrubs off. Her bra followed, then her trousers and shoes and pants, until she was standing naked in front of him.

He turned on the shower, stripped off his clothes and lifted her into the bath with him, pulling the curtain round them and holding her against him under the stream of hot water. After a moment she relaxed, and he reached for the shampoo, washed her hair and rinsed it and then soaped her, scrubbing her arms and hands to get rid of the memory of the blood.

She did the same for him, her fingers working through his scalp, running over his body, lathering him until he was so clean he nearly squeaked.

And then suddenly something changed, and they stood face to face under the stinging spray and their eyes locked.

'Oh, lord, Julia, forgive me,' he said raggedly, and his mouth came down over hers and he kissed her with all the pent-up yearning of the last few weeks.

She kissed him back, pressing herself against him, winding her limbs around his and sobbing his name, and then he lifted her against him, propping her against the tiles and driving into her until she screamed his name and fell apart, her body convulsing around him, and she felt the heavy, pulsing throb of his climax as he spilled deep inside her with a shuddering cry.

For a long moment they stayed there, motionless under the stream of the shower, and then David lowered her gently to her feet and wrapped her hard against his chest, his lips pressed to her head.

'Are you all right?' he said gruffly, and she nodded against his chest.

In fact, she wasn't sure. Her legs felt like jelly, her heart was still racing and in the back of her mind was a nagging thought that wouldn't quite come into focus.

He turned off the water, stepped out of the bath and wrapped himself in a towel, then swathed her in another one and lifted her out like a child, settling her on his lap as he perched on the loo seat and rubbed her gently dry.

'I didn't mean that to happen,' he said softly. 'I'm sorry. And we didn't think about contraception.'

The thought focused.

'Ah,' she said. 'No.'

'I'm sorry. It didn't seem like a priority at the time. Are you likely to get pregnant?'

She shook her head. 'No. I've got a coil. I had it put in after Katie, and I've never done anything about it. I suppose it's still all right.'

She felt the tension go out of him, and he hugged her gently against his chest.

'Good,' he said. 'And just in case you're worried, you won't catch anything from me. I've always been very careful.'

She stared at him, shocked. It had never occurred to her to think otherwise, and she realised how long she'd been out of circulation. 'David, I never even thought of it,' she said honestly.

'You should.'

'I've never needed to.'

He sighed and stroked her wet hair back from her face. 'Come on, let's get you dried and dressed and downstairs by the fire,' he murmured. Lifting her to her feet, he towelled her briskly and propelled her into the bedroom. It was chilly and she dressed quickly, suddenly shy of being naked in front of him.

Ridiculous after what had just happened, but nevertheless. Her body was nothing to write home about, her breasts changed by pregnancy and lactation, her abdomen still slightly curved below the waist from childbirth and lined here and there with stretch marks.

Andrew had been shocked at the change in her, and no amount of exercise or skin care had been able to eradicate the damage. David obviously hadn't seen it, but now suddenly Julia was desperately conscious of it and dragged her clothes on hastily before he could notice.

'I forgot socks,' she said in dismay, looking down at her cold feet.

'No problem.' He pulled open a drawer, fished out a pair of soft, thick socks and threw them at her. 'Right, let's get downstairs by that fire,' he said, tugging a jumper over his head and picking up another pair of socks for himself. He ushered her down to the sitting room, tucked her up by the fire and poured her a glass of wine, then pulled on his socks, went out to the kitchen and came back with a tray of bread and cheese and fruit cake.

'It's a bit scratch, but it'll fill a hole,' he said, and set it down on the toolbox. 'Tuck in.'

She did, suddenly starving, and when they'd eaten their fill and finished the wine he looked across at her and held out his hand.

'Come to bed with me,' he said, and the need she'd thought was slaked rose up again so that the breath jammed in her lungs and her heart skidded against her ribs. Putting her hand in his, she stood up with him and followed him up the stairs to his room.

Then the shyness came back, and when he'd stripped off his clothes she was still standing there fully dressed, her arms wrapped around her waist, her confidence fading by the second.

'Julia?' he murmured.

'Can we turn off the lights?'

He laughed softly. 'Why? You're lovely. I want to see you.'

'I'm not lovely,' she protested. 'My boobs droop and my stomach sags and I've got stretch marks...'

He laughed at her, just for a moment, then he realised she was serious and he drew her stiff, unyielding body into his arms and rocked her hard against his chest.

'Oh, you silly girl. That isn't what it's all about. Come on.'

'Please. I want the light off.'

'OK.'

He turned the top light off, but left the landing light on and the door open slightly, so they could see to move around the room. She turned away and removed her clothes, then slid between the chilly sheets with a shiver.

'Are you OK?' he asked, but she shook her head.

'It's been such an awful day,' she said, the memories suddenly crowding back in the dark so that she wished she'd braved it and left the light on.

'You're freezing. Come here,' he said, and tucked her up against his powerful body. His leg wedged between hers, his lips tracked over her face and throat and down over her breasts, leaving a trail of fire in their wake, and by the time he returned to her mouth she was shuddering with need.

David moved over her, his body trembling with passion held in check, and then they were moving together, driving out the memories of the day and replacing them with warmth and life and strength.

Julia felt the first ripples of release wash over her and cried out, and his body shuddered in response, driving into her until the sensation swamped her and she sobbed his name over and over again as he arched against her with a wild cry.

Then he slumped onto her, shifting his weight so he lay slightly to one side, his chest heaving against hers and his heart thundering in the aftermath of release.

Still locked together, they lay silent as their bodies calmed and slowed, and then, still together, drifted into sleep.

CHAPTER NINE

JULIA woke to the warmth of David's body and the firm, solid weight of his thigh between hers. They were sprawled together in his bed, face to face, and his hand lay by her breast, the back of it just grazing the sensitive skin as she breathed in and out.

As if he'd been waiting, his eyes opened and his lips quirked into a contented smile.

'Hi, gorgeous,' he murmured, and his voice was gruff with sleep and tantalised her.

'I have to go to work,' she told him, and he groaned and pulled her into his arms.

'No,' he grumbled gently.

'Yes.'

His sigh was deep, the breath teasing her hair. 'What time is it?'

'I don't know.'

He shifted, just far enough to turn his head and look at the clock. 'Oh, hell. It's only five-thirty. Ten more minutes.'

226

He nuzzled into the side of her neck, and she felt the familiar stirrings of desire deep inside her.

'No,' she said, pushing him away with a breathless little laugh.

'Yes.'

'I need a shower.'

He gave a gusty sigh and rolled away from her onto his back, his arm flopping above his head. 'Go on, then. I'll follow you.'

She slid out of the bed into the morning chill and went through to the bathroom. There was no lock, but it didn't worry her. She didn't think there was any way he was going to stir for at least another half-hour.

The bathroom was warm, courtesy of the heated towel rail, and she turned on the shower and stepped into the stinging spray. Wonderful. She turned her face up to the water and stood there for a moment, and then let out a tiny shriek of surprise as David's arms slid round her from behind.

She relaxed against him, relishing the feeling of his warm, hard body against her back.

'This is becoming a habit,' she scolded softly, and he chuckled and buried his lips in her hair.

She tried to turn round but he wouldn't let her. Instead he picked up the soap and lathered her, his hands tracing her body intimately until she was whimpering with need and her legs were giving way. She felt the first shock waves start to wash over her, and then he turned her, lifting her against him and driving into her as the climax ripped through her.

He staggered, his body shuddering in release, and then lowered her gently to her feet, his arms wrapped round her, her head tucked under his chin so she could hear the pounding of his heart and feel the rise and fall of his deep chest as his breathing slowed and he recovered.

Then he eased away from her and bent his head, taking her lips in a lingering kiss under the pelting water of the shower. It streamed over them but they ignored it until they couldn't breathe, then they broke apart, laughing, and he smoothed the rivers of hair from her face and kissed her again, just lightly.

'I love you,' he said, and the water seemed to turn to ice.

Julia backed away, his words echoing in her head, and reality slammed home.

What was she *doing?* She'd never meant to let things go so far, and now here they were, in the shower again, and David was telling her he loved her—

'No,' she said, her voice hollow with shock and panic. 'No, you don't.'

'Yes, I do.'

'No. No, really, you don't. It's just sex, David. That's all. Just sex.'

He stared at her for a moment, stunned, then shut off the water and stepped out of the shower, throwing her a towel.

'Don't be stupid. It's far more than that.'

'No,' she said, shaking her head again in denial. 'You're wrong. It's just hormones— just a basic human urge. Believe me, I know.'

'Really?' he said, and his voice was hard and cold. 'Surely, if it was *just sex* I'd go for a nubile, pert eighteen-year-old, not a widowed mother of nearly thirty who's got droopy boobs and a sagging stomach and stretch marks.'

She recoiled, her hand flying up to cover her mouth, and he shook his head in disgust.

'Your words, not mine,' he said, jabbing a finger at her. 'But you might want to think about it.'

'You bastard,' she whispered, pain ripping through her, tearing her apart. It was Andrew all over again, pouring scorn on her body, shredding her confidence, using her—

'No, I'm not the bastard,' he said, his voice still harsh, but then he let out his breath on a ragged sigh. 'I'm not here for sex, Julia, I'm here for love, because I love you, not your body—not that there's anything wrong with your body—'

'Liar,' she cut in savagely. 'Don't backtrack. You said what you meant.'

'No, I said what you said. And anyway, it's irrelevant. Whatever your body might or might not be like, did you notice me having trouble finding you attractive last night? Or again this morning?'

'You couldn't see me last night.'

'I didn't need to—I just needed to feel you, and you felt fine. You felt wonderful. You felt like you—and I love you.'

Her hands flew up to cover her ears. 'No!' she wept, not daring to believe him and be led once again into that tangled web of lies. 'I don't want to hear it!'

'Tough. It's not my fault. And don't blame me for loving you, it's not something I have any control over. But I do love you, and it's real. I won't lie and pretend otherwise just because you feel threatened by it. I'm sorry.'

She sank down onto the edge of the bath, the horror of what they'd done washing over her again and again. 'I didn't want this,' she said in a strangled whisper. 'I knew it was wrong. I knew this would happen.'

David flung the towel at the rail and turned to her, hands on hips, his beautiful body rigid with tension. 'You should have thought of that before, then, instead of encouraging it and leading me on and allowing it to happen,' he said savagely. 'You're not the only one that can get hurt, you know. I'm vulnerable too—just like anyone else.'

His eyes were locked with hers, the anger in them terrifying her. She felt tears spill down her cheeks, and dashed them away. 'I never meant to do this,' she said brokenly. 'I really didn't.'

'No,' he said, his voice deadly quiet, 'nor did I. It's a pity I didn't listen to you—a pity we ever met—but don't worry. The lesson's well learnt.'

He yanked open the door, letting in a stream of frigid air. 'Get dressed. I'm taking you home.'

They were mercifully busy at work. Ridiculously busy for a weekend, but extra staff had been called in to deal with the aftermath of the scaffolding collapse, and they could just about cope.

There was no time, though, for idle chat. No time for anyone to look closely at Julia and think anything other than that she looked tired and shocked. They knew she'd been at the scene of the collapse and had helped all day in Theatre, and any doubts anyone might have had about her cheerfulness could easily be blamed on that.

It was just as well. She felt as if the slightest word, the merest glance would reduce her to tears. All day she waited to hear David's voice, convinced he'd come in to see his patients of the day before, but he didn't. He stayed resolutely away, and she told herself she was glad.

She lied. She ached for him, on this day of all days, the anniversary of Andrew's death. It had been just as dawn had broken on the morning of the twenty-third of December four years ago that the police had come to tell her he was dead.

And as dawn had broken today, so her heart had shattered all over again.

Fool, she thought. It's taken you four years to put your life back together, four years to get things on track, and you have to go and do this!

She'd have to change her job, of course. She couldn't work with David, not now. It wouldn't be fair on either of them. Perhaps she'd move back towards her parents, she thought, or maybe down to Hampshire. No, not

Hampshire. She couldn't afford the house prices.

She thought of Katie's school friends, of Andrew's parents who for all their faults loved their little granddaughter to bits, and she thought of her friends and colleagues. She couldn't leave them all behind. Not again.

And now he wouldn't teach her about the garden, she thought, and that last silly little thing was the straw that broke the camel's back.

Sally Kennedy found Julia sobbing in the sluice and, assuming it was because of the strain of the day before, she sent her home early. Not very. It was nearly two, only just over an hour before the end of her shift, but she was all in.

The day before had taken its toll and, coupled with a lack of sleep and the emotional parting from David that morning, it was enough to send her straight to bed the moment she got home.

She found three messages on her answering machine from the Revells who had heard about the accident in the shopping precinct, and rang them to assure them she was all right.

'Could you keep Katie until tomorrow for me, though?' she asked. 'I know it's a nuisance, but I have to work in the morning and I had a horrendous day yesterday—I didn't get my day off at all. I'd really appreciate the rest.'

'Of course,' Mrs Revell said. 'Today, of all days, we'll keep her with us.'

Julia closed her eyes. They were grieving, of course, for their son, the apple of their eye, the man who in their eyes had done no wrong.

Well, maybe he hadn't. Maybe it had been her all along, in which case David would thank her in the end.

She hung up and crawled into bed, waking in the night to an unidentified hollow ache. Then she remembered, and the pain crashed over her again and nearly swamped her.

She rose early next morning and bathed, put on make-up to cover the ravages of her tears and went to work absurdly early.

Angie was pleased to see her. They were still running flat out and had been all night, and she joined in with the morning drug round and the taking of the obs. She took report, Angie handed her the keys and went off duty, and she carried on with all the million and one things that still needed doing, dispensing brittle little smiles right and left and hanging on by a thread.

And then David appeared.

She was just coming out of Mr Burrows's room, and her stride faltered for a second. His mouth was tight and he looked straight through her.

'Good morning, Sister,' he said quietly, his voice devoid of emotion.

She swallowed the obstruction in her throat. 'Good morning,' she managed, amazed that she managed to speak at all.

'How is Mr Burrows?'

Mr Burrows. Oh, lord. How was he? She made herself concentrate. 'Improving. His bowel sounds have returned. He's had sips of water and he's tolerating it well.'

He nodded. 'We can try him on something bland today. Nothing much—low residue liquid feed, I think.'

'Right. I'll sort that out.'

'And you can remove the catheter—see if we can get his bladder working properly again. Is he walking yet?'

Walking? Oh, lord. 'Um—yes. With assistance. He's walked round the room.'

'Good. Right, I'd better have a word.'

He stood in front of her, and after an agonised second she collected herself and moved out of his way so he could go through the door. She took another second to compose her face before following him, and conjured up a smile for Mr Burrows.

While David talked to him and examined him, she stood motionless, hanging onto her control by a thread. She'd known he'd be cool to her. She'd expected it, and she'd expected it to hurt. She'd just had no idea it could hurt so much.

She forced herself to concentrate.

'I don't suppose there's any chance I could go home for Christmas?' Mr Burrows was saying.

David glanced at his watch, his face expressionless. 'Christmas—that's tomorrow.' He sounded almost bemused, and after a second he seemed to shake himself slightly. 'Um, I don't know if that would be a good idea. You aren't well enough to be discharged.'

'Oh, I know that,' Mr Burrows said quickly. 'I just wondered, well, if I could go home for the day, or part of it.' He hesitated, then added in a low voice, 'It might be my last Christmas.'

David nodded slowly. 'Yes. I'm sorry. Yes, I think you could. I think you should. Go in the morning—about ten or so. Have a very quiet day, and come back before six. We'll give you the special diet and any pills you'll need during the day, but so long as your bladder's working and your bowel is comfortable, I don't see why not.'

The man's face crumpled with relief. 'Thank you,' he said with sincerity. 'Thank you so much. I was dreading tomorrow.'

David straightened his shoulders, stiffening slightly, and Julia felt another arrow of pain. Mr Burrows wasn't the only one dreading it.

'Right. Well, have a good Christmas. I'll see you on Boxing Day—and don't overdo it.'

'I won't. And Merry Christmas to you, too.'

'Thank you.' David turned on his heel and nearly fell over Julia. His hands came up instinctively to steady them both, but then he dropped her like a hot brick and exited the room with a muttered apology.

'He seems a bit preoccupied today,' Mr Burrows said thoughtfully, looking after him with a puzzled frown.

'I expect he's just busy,' Julia said. 'A lot to do before the holiday period.'

She straightened the sheets, flashed Mr Burrows what she hoped would pass for a smile and shot into the kitchen. She was trembling from top to toe, her cheeks were chalk white and she looked as if she'd seen a ghost.

The Ghost of Christmas Past? Or Christmas Present?

Which reminded her, she still hadn't got anything for Katie. Damn. And she was coming home at one, just after Julia got home from work, so there would be no time to shop for her before then.

They'd have to go to town that afternoon, and she'd have to let Katie choose her own present, unless she could lose her for a moment and do it surreptitiously.

She looked at her watch. Nine-thirty. Just two and a half hours to go before she was off duty and could escape.

Well, she couldn't hide in the kitchen for the entire morning, no matter how much she might want to. She drank a glass of cold water, straightened her shoulders and walked out of the door—slap into David.

'I was looking for you,' he said. His voice was strained and his eyes were fixed somewhere in her hairline. Far from looking *for* her, she thought, he was hardly even looking *at* her. Then he held something out to her, something hard and square, wrapped in Christmas paper with a little shiny red bow on top. 'This is for Katie,' he said. 'It's a mug with retriever puppies on it. Perhaps you could give it to her for me—and, ah, say goodbye.'

He thrust it into her hands and turned on his heel, striding away, his shoulders rigid, his hands rammed down into the pockets of his coat.

She stared after him, her throat aching, and then her eyes dropped to the parcel in her hands. He'd bought her daughter a present, and not just any present. Not a plastic toy or an inappropriate book or a jumper that didn't fit, but a mug with her beloved puppies on it.

A tear slipped down her cheek, and she stared down at her feet and blinked hard. Don't cry, she told herself. Not here. Don't start, you won't be able to stop. Just hang on.

'Julia?'

A pair of feet appeared beside hers, and she looked up at Sally.

'Oh, love, is it David?' she asked, and Julia nodded.

'Don't be nice to me. Whatever you do, don't be nice to me.'

Sally gave a crooked little grin. 'OK, I won't. Mrs Harrison's bowel appears to be working again—she's just had explosive diarrhoea through her stoma and overflowed the bag. Want to give me a hand?'

Julia laughed a little unsteadily. 'Oh, wow, I can hardly wait. Yes, I'll give you a hand. Let me put this in my locker.'

She rejoined Sally at Mrs Harrison's bed-side, and together they tidied her up and comforted her. The poor woman was acutely embarrassed and upset, and Julia put her problems aside and concentrated on convincing her that it didn't matter and nobody minded and once her tummy settled down it wouldn't be a regular feature of having a colostomy.

'Anyway,' she said, 'it's probably only for a short while until your bowel's healed, and then you can have it reversed.'

'Oh, I can't wait,' Mrs Harrison said miserably. 'I just hate this so much. I can't believe it's happening to me.' She started to cry again, and Julia hugged her and settled her down again for a rest.

Then she phoned Nick Sarazin and told him about the return of bowel function, and he said he'd come and talk to her as she was so unhappy, and see if he could cheer her up before Christmas.

He appeared a few moments later, chatted to Mrs Harrison for a few minutes and then came and found Julia.

'I've said I'll reverse the colostomy before Easter at the latest. I just hope I don't get struck down for lying to her, but hopefully the timescale will be all right.' He paused and peered at Julia closely. 'Hell, you look a bit rough. I gather you were caught up in the chaos on Saturday—are you all right?'

She nodded, glad that he'd taken the obvious line and not enquired more closely. 'I'll be OK after a couple of days off.'

'Hmm. David's looking pretty grim as well. It must have been a hell of a day. Are you spending Christmas together?'

She busied herself at the desk. 'No—he's got a big family do on. Katie and I are having a quiet Christmas on our own.'

'You can't!' he exclaimed. 'Oh, Julia! If we weren't going away I'd say come to us for the day. Isn't there anywhere you can go?'

She dredged up a smile. 'We'll be fine. Don't worry about us, we're OK. We're used to it.'

'Well, if you're sure,' he said doubtfully, but she was saved by his bleep going off. She handed him the phone and made herself scarce before his searching eyes delved a little deeper and came up trumps.

Then, finally, it was twelve o'clock and she could go off duty. She left the ward in a hail of Christmas greetings, and made her way home through the busy traffic. Everyone, it seemed, was knocking off early.

She showered and changed when she got home, and then at a quarter past one the doorbell rang and Katie skipped in, laden with presents and smiling from ear to ear.

'Thank you so much for keeping her the extra night,' Julia said to Mrs Revell. 'Have you had a lovely time, Katie?'

Her daughter nodded furiously. 'We did so many things! We went to see Father Christmas, and we had tea in town, and we put the presents under the tree and opened them yesterday morning— Have we got a tree yet, Mummy? Can we do it later?'

'We're going to get one this afternoon,' Julia promised. 'We have to go to town—I didn't get my shopping done on Saturday.'

'You won't get anything now, dear,' Mrs Revell said, looking disapproving. 'You should have started earlier. I'd done mine by October.'

'Well, I hadn't,' Julia said as evenly as she could manage. 'So, if you don't mind, we need to get on because time is now very short, as you've pointed out. Thank you so much. Katie, say thank you, darling.'

The child hugged her grandmother, kissed her goodbye and turned to Julia expectantly. 'Are we going now?'

'Yes—right this minute. Have you had lunch?'

She nodded, and so Julia put her coat on, scooped up her bag and keys and they headed down into town on foot. There was no point trying to take the car, and it was only a short walk.

The precinct was nearly deserted today, the scaffolding all cleared away and the shopfronts boarded up where the glass had been broken. It seemed like a ghost town, Julia thought. The blood had all been washed away, but she could still hear the screams and the weeping, and propped up against the shop that had been most badly affected were several bouquets of flowers.

Three people had died in there, two others under the scaffolding, and the tragedy seemed to hang in the air. People fell silent as they passed the site, and in the surrounding shops business was far from brisk.

They went into a big department store that seemed to have escaped from the sombre atmosphere of the street. 'So, what did Granny and Grandpa get you for Christmas?' she asked Katie as they wandered round through the last-minute crowds.

'Oh, lots,' she said, and rattled off a list of things, several of which had been on Julia's list of possibles and many more too expensive to be in reach of her budget.

Her heart sank. They walked out into the street again, to find that the Salvation Army band and choir were standing outside. They were singing 'In the Bleak Midwinter,' and as Julia and Katie went past, the choir sang the words, 'What can I give Him, poor as I am?'

The words struck a chord with Julia in her desperation. What can I give my daughter? she thought. Not my heart—she has that already and, anyway, just at the moment it's not really worth having. Oh, David…

They passed the shop with the print of Little Soham in it, and she hesitated outside. She still wanted to buy it for him—and they had another picture, too, of puppies playing in the snow. It was only a modern print, nothing special, but the puppies looked just like the ones at the Armstrongs' farm, and she knew Katie would love it.

'Oh, look, there's Father Christmas!' Julia said, pointing to a jolly man in the usual red garb with a flowing cotton-wool beard and red cheeks and a wonderfully padded stomach. 'I tell you what. I want to go into this shop for a minute. Why don't you stand here in the doorway and watch him, just for a second, all right?'

Katie nodded, and followed her into the shop, standing just inside the doorway while Julia had a murmured conversation with the man behind the counter.

One eye on her daughter, she pointed out the old print of Little Soham and the one of the puppies.

'Could you wrap them for me, please?' she asked, rummaging for her cheque book. 'My daughter's just standing over there, I don't want her to see.'

'Sure.' The man whipped the puppy picture down behind the counter, and then wrapped the two together in bubble wrap and brown paper.

'Thank you so much,' Julia said, hugely relieved that she'd found something suitable. She wrote out the cheque, told herself not to think about the cost and turned, pictures under her arm, Katie's name on her lips, but the doorway was empty.

'Katie?' Pushing past the people in the shop, she went out into the street and looked up and down, but there was no sign of her.

'Katie?' she called, telling herself to be calm, but the panic was starting to rise and she ran back into the shop, frantically calling and searching amongst the racks of prints.

'Are you looking for a little girl?' a woman asked her. 'The one with blonde curly hair?'

'Yes—she's five. Nearly six. She's got a blue coat on.'

'She went out, just a minute ago, while you were at the counter.'

Oh, God. Oh, please, God, no.

Julia ran back out into the street, calling Katie at the top of her voice, but there was nothing.

A policeman heard her calling and came over to her. 'Have you lost someone, madam?' he asked, and she looked up at him and started to shake.

'My daughter,' she said. 'I can't find my daughter. One minute she was there, the next she was gone. I told her to stand there. She was looking at Father Christmas—'

'Small girl, blonde hair, blue coat?'

She nodded in relief. 'Yes. Yes, that's her. Where is she?'

The policeman's face creased in a frown. 'She went with the man—Father Christmas. She was talking to him, and they went off together. I assumed she knew him.'

Julia stared at him in horror. 'She went with him? But she didn't know him! She'd never seen him before! Where did they go?'

But the policeman was already on the radio, calling for help to locate them. 'Don't worry, madam, we'll have her found in an instant,' he assured her, but she didn't believe him.

Her legs were trembling, her heart was pounding and there was a roaring in her ears. 'Katie,' she whispered desperately, her eyes still scanning the street. 'Katie, come back. Where are you?'

But there was no sign of her, or of the man dressed as Father Christmas who'd used the disguise to prey on her innocence and lead her goodness knows where. As the significance of her disappearance started to sink in, Julia's terror threatened to choke her. She could hardly breathe, bile was rising in her throat and the trembling spread to her whole body so she was racked with violent shudders.

Police were arriving, asking her questions, putting her in a patrol car and driving slowly along the precinct in the direction the pair had been seen to take.

Still no sign, no word, nothing. No one had seen them, nobody knew anything. Then a Father Christmas outfit was reported abandoned in a litter bin in the multi-storey car park, and Julia's world fell apart.

'We'll take you back to the station, madam, and start looking through the security videos from the CCTV cameras around the town,' the policeman sitting in the front of the patrol car suggested. 'Maybe we can pick something up. If you wouldn't mind coming to help us, we can probably pick her out easier with your assistance.'

'Oh, no,' she said, her hand over her mouth. 'I need to be in the town in case she comes back, looking for me.'

'Don't worry about the town—we've got people on the lookout for anyone answering her description. Do you have a picture of her?'

A picture? 'Yes—yes, I do, her school photo. It's in my bag.' She unzipped the little back pocket in her bag and pulled out the picture. Katie's bright, smiling face was shining up at her, and the happy image was more than she could stand. Would she ever see her again?

Julia started to cry, huge racking sobs that tore through her body, and the WPC next to her put her arms round her and held her tight.

'Don't worry, we'll find her,' she promised, but they were just empty words, and everyone knew it.

They pulled up at the police station and went inside, and someone asked for tea. 'Is there anyone we can call for you?' the policeman from the car asked, and she replied without thinking.

'David,' she said. 'I need David.'

They handed her a phone, and she phoned the hospital and asked them to page him. When he answered, he sounded wary. 'What is it?' he asked, his voice tight, and her courage almost failed her, but then she thought of Katie, and she knew she couldn't do this alone.

'Are you finished there?' she asked him.

'Just about. Why? Changed your mind? I can't deal with this, Julia. Not now. Not here. Besides, I didn't think there was anything left to say—'

'It's not me,' she said hurriedly, terrified that he'd hang up. 'Please, David, listen to me. It's Katie. She's gone missing, in town. David, someone's taken her, and I don't think I'll ever get her back!'

CHAPTER TEN

THERE was silence for a moment, then David said, 'Where are you?'

'The police station. David, hurry.'

'Stay there. I'm coming,' he told her, and the phone went dead.

Julia didn't know how she got through the next few minutes. Somehow saying it out loud had made it all much more real, and a terror she'd never imagined swept over her. She remembered thinking that if she could just lose Katie for a minute, she might be able to buy her a surprise present, but she'd never meant this—

'We need to look through this video first,' someone was saying to her. 'Tell us if you recognise her.'

She tried to focus, but her eyes were dry and unblinking and she could hardly see. People milled about in front of the camera, but because of the angle it was difficult to work out what she was seeing anyway. A great feeling of helplessness threatened to swamp her—helplessness and guilt, because if she hadn't taken her eyes off her…

'This is the shop you were in,' the man told her, pointing out a doorway, and gradually it began to make sense. 'Now, we had the call from PC Oswald about ten minutes after this, so it should be possible to see you go into the shop. How long do you think you were in there?'

She shook her head numbly. 'I don't know. Not long. I knew what I wanted and there wasn't a queue. I just bought two pictures.'

'So we might see you on this piece of film—there. Is that you?'

Was it? Possibly. 'I think so—and there's the Father Christmas that we saw.'

'Excellent. So, we're in the right place on the tape. All we have to do is keep watching.'

There were voices behind her, and she turned just as David came into the room.

'Julia,' he said, and his face looked so dear and familiar that she burst into tears.

His arms were round her, holding her up against his firm, solid chest, and his hands were rubbing her shoulders soothingly and holding her close.

'I didn't think you'd come,' she wept. 'Oh, David, help me. We have to find her.'

'We'll find her,' he said, but although she wanted to believe him, in a town the size of Audley, what hope did they have of finding one small girl before it was too late?

'What can we do?' he asked the police over her head.

'Not much, at the moment. We're screening video footage from the CCTV cameras around the area and in the car park where the costume was found.'

'Costume?' he asked.

'Father Christmas. The man dressed up as Father Christmas.'

'And so she trusted him,' he said slowly. 'Oh, my love.' His arms tightened, and she clung to him and dragged him down onto the seats.

'We have to look for her,' she said, her voice brittle with desperation. 'On the videos.

We've just found the bit where we go into the shop.'

They watched impatiently as the Father Christmas stooped to talk to the little children that passed, and then suddenly there she was, her Katie, her little face turned up trustingly to the cheerful figure in red.

'That's her,' Julia said. 'That's Katie.' She had a death-like grip on David's hand, and he put his other arm round her and held her tight. They watched in silence as the man held out his hand, and Katie slipped her little hand into it and went with him without question.

The police team worked on the images, re-fining them as much as possible, but it wasn't good enough to get any idea of the identity of the abductor. With the heavy disguise it was impossible to see more than just the eyes, and they were too indistinct to be of any use.

Then David stiffened and leant forwards to get a better view.

'Look,' he said. 'That hand—it doesn't look like a man's hand, and that person's not very big, you know. Katie's deceptively small—you compare them to the other people around them.

I don't think it's a man at all. I think it's a woman.'

They looked again, studying the film over and over, and Julia nodded slowly. 'You're right. That person doesn't walk like a man. There's too much sway of the hips. Men don't walk like that, and Katie would look smaller beside a man, anyway, unless it was a very small man.'

'Right. I want the women checked,' Tony Palmer, the detective in charge, snapped. 'Any woman with a record of abduction or anything similar, anyone with a psychiatric record—anything that might be even slightly relevant. Let's look through the car park footage again. We were looking for a man—we might have overlooked something.'

Please, Julia thought, let it be a woman. A woman might not hurt her—not so much. Not in that way. Oh, God, please, let it be a woman.

And then they found her. An ordinary woman, slim, dressed in jeans and a jumper, was ushering a child in front of her, stooping to talk to her. As she turned to unlock the car, they could just make out that the child was Katie. She seemed quite happy, and there was certainly no struggling. She got into the car without protest, and a moment later they drove away.

'Get that registration,' Tony Palmer snapped, and for the first time, Julia felt the first tiny stirrings of hope.

They had the number of the car, and with that number they could trace her.

They zoomed in on the video image and managed to get all but one letter of the registration. Julia's hope faded again, but David squeezed her hand. 'They'll get it. They know the make and colour of the car. That's enough.'

Did she dare to believe him? 'Please, hurry,' she said under her breath. 'Please, please, hurry.'

'Right, got it,' someone said a couple of minutes later. 'The car's registered to an Avril Brown—84 St Anne's Drive.'

'Right, let's go,' the team leader said, and held a hand out to them. 'You'd better come. If she's there, Katie will need you.'

The drive was a nightmare of sirens and flashing lights, but as they approached the house the sirens were turned off and they approached carefully.

Men ran round the back, others surrounded the front of the modest little semi-detached house, and then Tony Palmer rang the doorbell.

For a moment there was no response and Julia felt her hope draining away again, but then the door opened and a sad, mousy woman with hopeless eyes stood there on the step.

'She's here,' she said woodenly, and then Katie appeared at her side, a bedraggled teddy tucked under one arm, and beamed up at them, and Julia's thrashing heart nearly stopped dead with relief.

'Hello, Mummy,' Katie said excitedly. 'I've been watching telly and playing. Avril's one of Father Christmas's helpers—she has to dress up and talk to the children to help him, but she'd finished work today so we came back here, and she let me play with all sorts of toys. I said we should tell you, but she said you wouldn't mind. Did you mind, Mummy?'

Julia thought she'd fall apart, but David had a vice-like grip on her hand and from somewhere deep inside her came the strength to hang on.

'I was a bit worried,' she said, wondering how it was possible to make such a massive understatement without giving herself away. 'You should have stayed where I told you, you know.'

Her little face fell. 'I'm sorry,' she said. 'Mummy, come and see the toys. They were Jenny's. They're really nice.'

Jenny's? 'Not now, darling,' she said as steadily as she could manage. 'We have to go and decorate the tree—remember? And anyway, Avril's busy. The police need to talk to her.'

Katie looked around at all the police standing there, and her face creased in a little puzzled frown. 'Did she do something wrong?' she said, and beside her Avril started to cry.

'I never meant to hurt her,' she sobbed. 'I only wanted to talk to the children, but she was so like Jenny…'

'Jenny died,' Katie explained innocently. 'This was her teddy. Here...'

She pressed the teddy worriedly into Avril's hands, then reached up her little arms and pulled the woman down to kiss her. 'Bye,' she said. 'I have to go now. Thank you for having me.'

For a second the woman clung to her, then she let her go, and Katie ran down the path to Julia and took her hand. 'Can we go and do the tree now?' she said innocently, her guileless little face shining up at her mother.

'I think that's a good idea,' Julia said, trying not to give in to the urge to sweep her up into her arms. She couldn't believe Katie was back with her and unharmed. It was like waking from a nightmare, but finding you were still in the place you'd dreamed of.

They sat in the back of the police car, her and David with Katie in between them, and drove back to the police station while Katie chatted happily about Avril and Jenny and the toys, and all Julia could think was that Katie was alive and poor little Jenny was dead, and how sad Avril had looked.

'That poor woman,' she murmured, and David squeezed her arm supportively.

'Are you all right?' he mouthed, and she nodded.

Yes. Yes, she was all right. Katie was alive and unharmed. Nothing else mattered.

At the police station it was agreed that they should go home and that a WPC with special training with children should come and talk to them on Boxing Day to get Katie's story, although it seemed fairly cut and dried from the video evidence and what she'd already said.

'It's just a formality, really,' Tony Palmer explained, 'and with it being Christmas, we don't need to do it now.'

'I'll be at home,' Julia said, but David cut in.

'No. She'll be with me at my family home for the next few days. I'll give you the address and the phone number.'

'Really?' Katie said, bouncing on the spot. 'Are we going there for Christmas?'

'Would you like that?' he asked, and she nodded vigorously.

'Will the puppies still be there? Can I still play with them?'

'Of course you can, half-pint. They'll be expecting you.' He ruffled her hair, and she giggled and put her arms around his hips and hugged him as he jotted down the details of the farm.

Julia stared at him, torn between wanting to be near him and the need to maintain her independence at all cost. 'But—David—you don't want us—'

'Don't tell me what I feel,' he said, his voice deathly quiet. 'And anyway, it's irrelevant. You aren't spending Christmas alone, and that's that. Besides, they'd have my guts for garters if I didn't take you there.'

She didn't bother to protest. She didn't want to be alone with Katie, her feelings were too fragile, and she didn't want to turn what seemed to have been a pleasant experience into one of horror for the child by overreacting.

And Christmas with David's warm and loving family would be just what they all needed.

If only things hadn't gone so badly wrong at the weekend, she thought. If only things hadn't got out of hand and propelled them into that wild and tempestuous physical relationship, then they could still have been friends, instead of hurting each other and making the situation impossible.

Still, their feelings didn't matter at the moment. It was Katie she was concerned about, and she and David were both old enough to put their relationship on one side for the sake of the child.

'Don't forget your parcel, Mrs Revell,' the WPC said as they were leaving, and handed her the pictures that had caused all the trouble. 'Have a good Christmas. I'm so glad everything worked out all right.'

Julia hugged her, grateful for her support during the ordeal. 'Thank you. You've given me the best present in the world,' she said emotionally, looking round at them all. 'Thank you all so much.'

'Our pleasure. You take care, now,' Tony Palmer said.

She hesitated. 'About Avril—she needs help.'

He nodded. 'We'll see to it. She'll be all right, don't worry about her. You get on home now and have your Christmas. We'll see you afterwards.'

David ushered them out into the car and strapped Katie into the car seat, while Julia tried to fasten her own seat belt with fingers that trembled with reaction.

'Let me,' he said, sliding in beside her. 'Are you all right?'

She nodded. She didn't dare speak for a moment, and he squeezed her hand in understanding and started the car.

'Right, let's go to your house and pick up some things for you on the way,' he said briskly.

She hadn't even thought of it. There were a million things she hadn't thought of, but none of them mattered. She dropped her head back against the headrest and let him take over.

'Here we are,' he said, dredging up a smile for Katie's benefit. 'Have you got your keys?'

She nodded. 'Do your parents know what's happening?'

He cut the engine. 'I rang them on the way to the police station and told them what had happened. I need to phone them and tell them we've found her.'

'Call them from my house while I pack,' she suggested, and he nodded.

As she ran upstairs with Katie to gather their things together, he went into the kitchen, picked up the phone and dialled the number. His fingers were trembling slightly, and at the sound of his mother's voice he had to swallow hard before he could speak.

'She's all right, we've got her back and we're coming over,' he said gruffly.

'Oh, darling,' his mother said, and burst into tears. His father came on the line, more controlled but no less anxious, and David appealed to them for calm at the house.

'Katie's fine, but she's totally unaware of the havoc she's caused. I'll tell you all about it when we get there, but just don't say anything, all right? All she can talk about is playing with the puppies.'

'Fine. I'll prime them all. We'll expect you soon.'

He put the phone down and closed his eyes, breathing slowly and deeply and struggling for control. He had to be strong for Julia and for Katie—and if she could do it, so could he.

He couldn't believe how controlled she'd been when Katie had come out of the door. He would have grabbed her and run, and as for her attitude to Avril—where did she find so much compassion? He would have killed the woman for taking his daughter, and if Katie had been harmed, his daughter or not, he probably would have done so.

But she hadn't been harmed, and it was all going to be all right, and all he had to do was get through the next few days without falling apart.

They arrived at the farm shortly before six, only three hours after Katie had disappeared. It had been the longest three hours of Julia's life, and nothing could have prepared her for the agony of that wait.

Still, it was over, and all she wanted was to put it behind her. She walked slowly down the path to the front door, Katie running ahead and throwing herself into Mrs Armstrong's waiting arms, and she looked at Julia over the child's head and smiled tearfully.

'Hello, my dear,' she said, and putting Katie down she drew Julia into a warm and motherly embrace. 'I'm so glad everything's all right,' she murmured, hugging her hard, and Julia hugged her back.

'Thank you.'

Mrs Armstrong held her at arm's length and studied her closely. 'Are you all right? You poor child, it must have been awful. Come inside—I expect Katie's in with the puppies already. She'll have to share them today, because David's sister's children are here. Jeremy, open a bottle of wine, we need to celebrate.'

And just like that they were absorbed into the warmth of the family. They all crowded round the big kitchen table for supper, with the three children sitting together across one end and the adults all squeezed up on odd chairs, and Julia was sandwiched between David and his mother and plied with food and drink.

She could see Katie bubbling with excitement, and gradually she felt the tension in her start to ease.

'She's fine,' David said, intercepting an anxious look, and she laughed unsteadily and nodded.

'Yes, she is. I know. Thank you—it wouldn't have been nearly so easy at home. You were quite right.'

'You ought to learn to trust me,' he said softly, and she looked into his beautiful quicksilver eyes and wished she could dare to believe in him.

Supper finally came to an end, and they all helped to clear the table and do the dishes. David's sister's husband washed, and his brothers and younger sister dried and put away and cleared the table. David went into the drawing room and put logs on the woodburner and went out to fill the log basket.

Julia found herself with Mrs Armstrong and David's sister, supervising the children so that the puppies didn't get too exhausted, and while they watched over them Mrs Armstrong said, 'Shall we put Katie in with the other two for the night? I'm sure they'd love to bunk up together, if you're both happy with that?'

'Sure, fine,' David's sister said, but Julia felt a moment of panic.

'Oh. I thought— Can't she share with me?'

David paused beside them. 'I thought you could have my room,' he said to Julia. 'There's a day-bed in the study. I'll sleep on that. The kids are just next to my room, so she wouldn't be far away, and she'll have more fun in with them. It'll keep her mind occupied, as well.'

Julia nodded. He was right, of course, but the thought of her being out of sight—

'She'll be safe,' Mrs Armstrong said softly. 'No harm will come to her in this house.'

She felt the tension ebb out of her. 'You're right. Of course you are. Yes, let her sleep with the others, she'll love it.'

And she herself would be in David's room. What sweet irony.

The children were packed off to bed by nine, protesting through their yawns, and then the Christmas stocking fillers came out.

'I wasn't sure if Katie would be here, so I got her a few things,' Mrs Armstrong explained. 'I don't know if you do the Christmas stocking thing, or if after today—well, maybe you don't want references to Father Christmas.'

But Katie had been happily telling everyone of her adventure with one of his helpers, so Julia didn't think it would do any harm.

Not to the child, at least, and nothing would remind Julia herself of the events of the day because there was no way they were out of her mind for more than an instant.

'I'm sure she'd love a stocking, she always has one at home,' Julia agreed, touched that Mrs Armstrong had thought of Katie in the midst of all her family preparations. And so had her son, of course. 'David gave me a present for her the other day,' she told them. 'Should I put it under the tree with all the others?'

'That would be nice for her.'

'And I need some wrapping paper—I don't suppose you've got any, have you? I've just got a couple of things to do.'

They found her some paper and tape and pretty bows, and she sat at the kitchen table and wrapped David's picture while Mrs Armstrong stood guard and made sure he didn't come in.

'Oh, it's perfect—how appropriate!' she said, looking over Julia's shoulder at the print of Little Soham. 'Oh, Julia, you clever girl, he'll love it.'

'I hope so,' she said wistfully. She wasn't convinced. She thought of all the terrible things they'd said to each other at the weekend, and wondered how he'd managed to be so kind to her today.

Still, maybe it was appropriate, as it had been his picture she'd been buying when Katie had disappeared. Well, his and Katie's, to be fair.

She finished wrapping it, did Katie's puppy picture and managed to slip them both under the tree ready for the morning while no one was looking. She just hoped no one else had given Katie anything, because she felt very guilty about having nothing to give any of the others after all their kindness.

Still, under the circumstances it was unlikely, she thought.

They spent the rest of the evening by the fire in the drawing room, with all the usual banter of a large family surrounding Julia and wrapping her in its warm friendliness, and then at eleven the party broke up and they started to drift off to bed. Mr Armstrong took the dogs out, Mrs Armstrong gave the puppies a last feed and cleared up after them, and the others all disappeared upstairs.

David's sister went off with the three Christmas stockings in hand to put on the children's beds, and David took Julia up to his room.

Her case was on the bed, and he showed her the switch for the bedside light, and asked if she wanted the window open or closed, and then he stopped talking and looked at her for a long, considering moment.

'Are you all right?' he asked gently, and she nodded.

Actually it was a lie. She suddenly felt very emotional and raw all over again, and as if he realised that, he took her hand and led her out onto the landing and opened the children's bedroom door.

'She's fine. Look—fast asleep.'

Katie was, absolutely out for the count, exhausted by all the fun she'd had that evening with the other two and all the puppies. Julia bent over her and pressed a gentle kiss to her cheek, and she sighed softly and rolled onto her side.

For a long moment she stared at her daughter, and then everything seemed to blur, and she stood up and stumbled blindly towards the door.

David's arm came round her shoulders and he led her back into his room, turning her into his arms and holding her while the scalding tears fell. Then he mopped her up and gave her a slightly strained smile.

'Better now?'

She nodded. 'I'm sorry. It's just been one of those awful days.' She bit her lip, and he cupped her face in his hands and brushed her tears away with his thumbs.

'I don't know how you've been so brave,' he said gruffly.

'I couldn't have done it without you,' she told him with painful honesty. She looked away, unable to meet his eyes after all the dreadful things she'd said. If only she could undo them, go back to the beginning of the end and stop them before everything had gone so horribly wrong—but she couldn't.

'Will you be all right?' he asked quietly.

She nodded. 'I think so. I'll have to be, won't I?'

'I'll say goodnight, then.'

She nodded again, and he opened the door and took one step through it before her courage deserted her.

'David?'

He stopped. 'What is it?' he asked softly.

'Stay with me,' she said in a rush. 'I know it's too much to ask, but I really can't face being alone. I'm sorry...'

He was motionless for a minute, then he let out his breath on a ragged sigh. 'Don't be sorry. I'll be back in a minute. You get ready for bed.'

He left her, and she changed quickly into her nightshirt. It was a little tired and washed out, but it was the only one she'd been able to find and anyway, it didn't matter. She wasn't trying to dress up for him.

She cleaned her teeth at the basin in the corner of the room, and then there was a knock on the door and David came in. He was dressed in pyjamas, and he hardly looked at her.

'All right?' he asked.

She nodded. 'I just need the bathroom.'

'It's next door,' he reminded her, and she slipped out of the room and glanced along the corridor. Would his parents object to them being together, she wondered, or would they be pleased? Not that it was significant. She'd dealt a death blow to any hopes she might have had in his direction.

David was sitting on the edge of the bed when she got back, and he looked up at her unsmilingly.

'Which side do you want?' he asked.

She shrugged. It didn't matter. She was so used to sleeping alone that either side would feel odd. 'I don't mind.'

'Then I'll have the left,' he said, and turned back the quilt for her. 'Get in—I'll put out the light.'

She slid between the cold sheets and lay down as he flicked off the light, then she felt the mattress dip as he got in beside her. For a moment all she could hear was her own heart-beat, loud in the silence, and the even, quiet sound of his breathing, then the bed shifted as he turned towards her and he reached out his arms.

'Come here,' he said gruffly, and she found herself enfolded in a warm and undemanding embrace. 'That's better. Now, go to sleep.'

'I can't. I keep thinking about today.'

'It's over, Julia. Let it go. She's safe.'

He was right, and she was suddenly ex-hausted. She let herself relax into his arms, and after a few seconds she felt sleep claim her.

It didn't last. She woke at some time in the middle of the night with a start, and slipped out of bed to check Katie. She stubbed her toe in the dark, and hobbled next door as quietly as she could, feeling relieved and yet foolish to find her daughter exactly as she'd left her.

'Is she all right?' David asked as she came back in.

'She's fine. I'm just being silly.'

'I don't think so. You've had a hell of a day.'

She slid back into bed and lay there, a few inches away from him, afraid to move closer in case he thought she assumed too much. She hoped he'd take her in his arms again, but he made no move towards her. Strangely dispirited, she fell asleep, but when she next woke it was to find herself in his arms once more, her head pillowed on his chest and their legs entangled.

'Are you OK?' he asked, and she realised he must have been awake. Watching over her? She didn't know, but it felt like it, and it was wonderful.

More than she deserved.

She thought of his kindness to her that afternoon, the way he'd dropped everything and come straight to her, giving her unquestioning support and never once telling her what she'd known, that she'd failed Katie by not watching her.

Andrew would have told her.

No. What was she thinking about? Andrew wouldn't have come near her, a widow with a child! No, he would have gone for the pert eighteen-year-old that David had talked about, like the girl he'd been with the night he'd died. There was certainly no way he would have come anywhere near her if she'd spoken to him the way she'd spoken to David on Sunday morning. His pride would have prevented it, but there was no sign of David's pride.

Just his compassion, and caring, and loyalty.

She swallowed hard. He wasn't anything like Andrew. She'd thought he was, because the sex had been so good and Andrew had always prided himself on his performance, but there had been no pride about David on Saturday night, just generosity and passion and honesty.

Maybe he really did love her? It seemed impossible that he could, but even more impossible that he didn't, given the way he'd behaved since. Not only did he love her, she realised, but he'd been there for her when she'd needed him in a way Andrew would never have been.

So, so different. How could she possibly have confused them? Fear, of course. Fear of another failure, of more pain and humiliation, fear for Katie, but there was nothing to fear from David.

She realised that, now it was too late.

But not too late to apologise.

'David?' she whispered.

'Mmm?'

'I'm sorry,' she said softly. 'I said some dreadful things to you the other day, and I was wrong about you—appallingly, horribly wrong. Can you forgive me?'

He was silent for a moment, then turned towards her, his hand coming up and cradling her cheek. 'There's nothing to forgive,' he said, his voice raw. 'You were frightened. I pushed you too hard—you weren't ready. And talking of forgiveness and saying dreadful things, I don't know why I was so cruel to you. I can't believe I said what I did about your body. It was totally uncalled for, even if they were your own words. I was just angry and hurt and I lashed out. I'm sorry.'

Her hand covered his in comfort. 'Don't be. And don't lie to me about it. I know it's no great shakes—'

'It's beautiful.'

She felt tears fill her eyes. 'Don't lie, please, David, don't lie,' she begged him, but he drew her closer into his arms and kissed her.

'I'm not lying. You're a wonderful woman, Julia. Brave and beautiful and strong and funny and sexy and tender, and if I wanted you any more than I do it would be dangerous for my health.' He kissed her again, then said quietly, 'Maybe it's just because I love you.'

Her heart sang with joy. She'd thought she'd never hear him say those words again, and they gave her the courage she needed. She lifted her hand and stroked his cheek, revelling in the rasp of his beard against her palm.

'I love you, too,' she said unsteadily. 'I have done almost from the moment we met. I didn't mean to. I didn't want to, because I didn't think you could ever return my love and I was afraid of hurting Katie, but I couldn't resist you. Now, though—I can understand if you don't want to know, I've been a bit slow on the uptake, but today I realised I can trust you. I just hope it's not too late for us. I want to be with you, share my life with you, have your children.'

She took a deep, steadying breath and went on, 'Marry me, David. Please?'

For an endless moment she thought he was going to refuse, then he took her lips in a searing kiss that erased any last shred of doubt she might have had.

'Oh, my sweet love, of course I'll marry you,' he said raggedly, and drew her back into his arms. 'I thought I'd lost you—thought it was all over and I'd blown it—but now we've got another chance. I didn't think we'd get that lucky. Let's not blow it this time, please?'

He made love to her then, not like the wild and passionate mating of the weekend, but slow and tender and infinitely gentle, and at the end she wept in his arms, and their tears mingled on her cheeks.

They fell asleep with their limbs still entwined, and awoke to the sound of the children giggling with delight and bouncing on the beds next door.

'Good grief, whatever time is it?' he mumbled gently.

'Time to get up?' she suggested, and he gave a strangled laugh and turned on the bedside light.

'It's not even six!'

'It's Christmas.'

He dropped back onto the pillow and groaned. 'Do we have to go down?'

She sat up and looked down at him, no longer worried about her nakedness. 'I think so. We've got something to tell them, haven't we?'

He smiled slowly. 'Absolutely.' He threw off the covers, retrieved his pyjamas from the foot of the bed and pulled them on, lobbing her nightshirt to her. 'Come on, stick that on with your dressing gown and let's go and tell them the news.'

They followed the sound of excited voices down the stairs, and found all the family gathered in the drawing room, trying to stall the children from opening the presents.

At the threshold David stopped her and drew Julia into his arms, glancing up at the mistletoe pinned to the beam above before kissing her lingeringly. 'Happy Christmas,' he said softly.

She thought of yesterday, and how she'd nearly lost everything that mattered to her in the world, and how now she had it all, and her lips softened in a smile of utter joy. 'Happy Christmas,' she echoed.

They turned towards the drawing room and found everyone had fallen silent, their eyes fixed on them with identical expressions of curious fascination.

'I hope that kiss means what I think it means,' Mrs Armstrong said searchingly, and David looked down at Julia for confirmation.

Over to you, he seemed to be saying. She looked at Katie, watching them with her head tilted to one side and a puzzled and slightly hopeful expression on her face.

'How do you fancy a new daddy?' Julia said, and Katie scrambled to her feet and ran over, looking up at them with shining eyes.

'Do you mean David?' she asked, and when he nodded, she squealed with delight and threw herself into his arms.

'I take it that's a yes,' he said with a chuckle, scooping her up against his chest. Julia looked up at him, at his laughing eyes and tender smile, and her daughter hugging him and raining kisses on his early morning stubble, and felt her heart swell.

The others were hugging them and pumping David's hand, his mother was in tears again, and Julia knew if she lived to be a hundred, there could never be a more perfect Christmas...

MEDICAL ROMANCE™

Large Print

Titles for the next six months…

July

DOCTOR IN DANGER	Alison Roberts
THE NURSE'S CHALLENGE	Abigail Gordon
MARRIAGE AND MATERNITY	Gill Sanderson
THE MIDWIFE BRIDE	Janet Ferguson

August

GUILTY SECRET	Josie Metcalfe
PARTNERS BY CONTRACT	Kim Lawrence
MORGAN'S SON	Jennifer Taylor
A VERY TENDER PRACTICE	Laura MacDonald

September

INNOCENT SECRET	Josie Metcalfe
HER DR WRIGHT	Meredith Webber
THE SURGEON'S LOVE-CHILD	Lilian Darcy
BACK IN HER BED	Carol Wood

MILLS & BOON®

MEDICAL ROMANCE™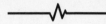

——√√—— *Large Print* ——√√——

October

A WOMAN WORTH WAITING FOR	Meredith Webber
A NURSE'S COURAGE	Jessica Matthews
THE GREEK SURGEON	Margaret Barker
DOCTOR IN NEED	Margaret O'Neill

November

THE DOCTORS' BABY	Marion Lennox
LIFE SUPPORT	Jennifer Taylor
RIVALS IN PRACTICE	Alison Roberts
EMERGENCY RESCUE	Abigail Gordon

December

A VERY SINGLE WOMAN	Caroline Anderson
THE STRANGER'S SECRET	Maggie Kingsley
HER PARTNER'S PASSION	Carol Wood
THE OUTBACK MATCH	Lucy Clark

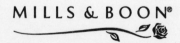

MILLS & BOON®